C000294660

Dear Alice,

This was written for fun to raise funds for Trinity — but also to entertain those who know, and love, "The Great Gatsby"

I do hope you might enjoy it!

Love
Ian

Oxford
January 2018.

GATSBY AT TRINITY

Ian Flintoff

PITCHFORK PRODUCTION

with

YOUCAXTON PUBLICATIONS

OXFORD & SHREWSBURY

Copyright © Ian Flintoff 2014

The Author asserts the moral right to
be identified as the author of this work.

ISBN 978-190964-469-4
Printed and bound in Great Britain.

Published by
Pitchfork Production,
5 Orchard Court,
Rose Hill,
Oxford OX4 4HJ
www.pitchforkproduction.com

All rights reserved. No part of this publication may be reproduced,
stored in a retrieval system, or transmitted in any form or by
any means, electronic, mechanical, photocopying, recording or
otherwise, without the prior permission of the publisher.

This book is sold subject to the condition that it shall not, by way of
trade or otherwise, be lent, resold, hired out or otherwise circulated
without the publisher's prior consent in any form of binding or cover
other than that in which it is published and without a similar condition
including this condition being imposed on the subsequent purchaser.

This was written for Deirdre
with love.

Also for John-Paul and Crispin,
who seek to inspire and do inspire.

For all my family and friends
and all the men and women
of Trinity College, Oxford,
a place I love and cherish.

With special acknowledgement to
Clare Hopkins
for her much valued help with this
and for her brilliant work as the Trinity archivist.

Presidents Norrington, Quinton,
Beloff, and Roberts
have all affected my life and loyalty to Trinity
in various ways,
as have Frank Barnett, Bryan Ward-Perkins
and Dick Cadman.

Richard de la Mare, Tom MacKeown
and Gordon Deighton
were special friends during my first Trinity days and
have remained much loved friends ever since.

Though the sky be too dark for dim eyes to discover
The gold hat and Daisy fair blooming thereunder.

(Jay Gatsby, with thanks to William Morris)

When you have read this book, please read *The Great Gatsby* again. You'll see why.

Good luck!

Ian Flintoff

Chapter 1

It was welcome. The time, I mean. The time – and the place.

My quest for identity – a thing doubted and much puzzled over, I suspect, in the years to come – was both clarified and blurred by the awakening months I spent in my new abode.

The proposal had come, as they say, out of the blue. Some of the people I was to meet would not only make more possible what I have sometimes called, to myself, "the white roadster" moment with Daisy, the fireside spell and all that followed it, including the horrifying news in her letter to Trinity – but they would also give me a determination and a taste for books and for writing, fostered under the wing of Trinity College, and which alone make this volume possible. That it is written at all, and if at all decently, is thanks to what Meyer calls Oggsford.

When this book is finished, I shall close it and never write again. Other than in these pages I shall make little of the events which took me first to Oxford instead of home, as I had intended, after my service was over in the war.

It is not that my days at Trinity College must be forgotten. No, it is that I must, when this is completed, create a person and a place for myself without a past as such. A glancing mention maybe, in later years, but nothing more. In the early days at Trinity I still owned the dream, the mystery of the sirens and the certainty of hope. It was also at Trinity that my sun exploded. Therefore this book is the only true record of what occurred between my fighting in France and the final and ruthless rush for wealth.

Before the military and before Trinity College I had often, with justice, been described as a young roughneck, a tough all-American boy, eager for the dream and careless of ways and means to achieve that dream.

There is truth in this and I am certain that if anyone were to write about me later, for whatever reason, I will be depicted as blunt, sharp, determined, one-tracked, sinister even, or mysterious – or perhaps as one who believes himself to be a son of God and obliged therefore to do his father's business.

There is also, however, my own story, the inner story, the Jay Gatsby I invented from within. This, once-for-all and ended, is that story, those months, that evolution.

"I have information, major, which may be of interest."

I noted the clerk did not call me sir – an indicator that the war was now over and that perhaps a period of calm, though less deference, would move into our lives in the months ahead. What could the 1920s and the 1930s hold? Peace and freedom to say the very least. And, to use yet another expression I would learn from my later English friends, I had "done my bit" to secure these certainties.

"What information is that, Cranby?"

"The note came to us from the White House. I gather it is intended to be just informal and in no way meant to be given publicity. As I understand it, President Poincaré first made the overture directly to President Wilson, and this was followed up by the English Prime Minister and then the Prince of Wales. The invitation is to all servicemen like yourself."

From what he told me it was a gesture of gratitude. My name, however, had already been confirmed as a participant, without my knowing and with no consultation. In principle, I learned, I had no choice. Returning home and finding her would therefore have to be delayed.

Only a few months before I had been with the Sixteenth Infantry Regiment of the First Division. We had taken part in every campaign of that First Division. The Sixteenth Regiment, my own, was the first to take American casualties and to engage with the Germans. More unforgettably, though I seldom endeavored to bring these things too vividly to mind, was the battle of Argonne Forest. This was to be my last battle until the armistice in November 1918. We lost one hundred and seventeen thousand Americans. I was lucky – though I had several friends who died, including Chuck Deacon. For what I did in that battle they promoted me to major and I was given medals. Every allied government gave me a decoration of some sort. Even Montenegro: from King Nicolas himself, the Orderi di Danilo.

These, I say, are events I would prefer to leave within the closed archives of the mind. Of far more value to me was the recollection of a time in October 1917, a time in Louisville, Kentucky, when the simple purpose of my life took its own final form and being, and this in a way which prevented all other purposes from dominance or competition.

I was a lieutenant then, due to sail to Europe and to fight.

It was in a white automobile, or roadster, in Louisville standing outside the house of the Fay family that an eternal premonition came upon me, this for the first and last time of my life. I would never lose that, never forget it, or ever disown it. Other incidents endorsed this, together by a fireside being one such. She became mine and I hers, fully as lovers, and both equal in that depth of giving.

It was true, though I now acknowledged this only with reluctance, that at one time I had hoped in a perverse way that she would leave me.

I was poor, poor as hell at that time. She and her family were rich, stylish, without questions. I had my lieutenant's uniform to disguise what I really was, and I could not but feel a little that I was a fraud, and that the girl took me for more wealth and status than was the case. But no! Her love, my love, our love were real and true – so all that remained for me to do was to transform the poor boy Gatz to the resplendent Gatsby.

I could not then have guessed the grieving nights I would later know in English lanes.

I had hoped for a recapture in New York of those earlier moments with her in Kentucky, to meet before I was to leave for France, yet somehow it did not happen. She did not come. No matter. With the war now ended, I knew the need to seek the special new identity and also the practical means to consolidate that need.

"Any university you choose," Cranby explained. "Your name has been committed, I'm afraid. Presidential generosities cannot be slighted."

He was no longer in the military but had volunteered his services with personnel liaison. We were together now, in a special office for the purpose of rehabilitation, at 39 Whitehall Street in Manhattan, New York. The building was an American pride of red granite and Portland Lake sandstone, with a stained glass dome reminiscent of the Old World to which, at this second of further commitment, I was about to choose to return.

"Any university in France or England. There's the Sorbonne and Montpellier, for instance. Or there are

Cambridge, Oxford and St Andrew's – though that's in Scotland, I understand. You can, as they say, take your pick. You will have to go though, I'm afraid, major. Your name has been registered, irreversibly."

Well, why not? I had intended to go to Louisville, to find her, to be there. I would write to her and she would wait and understand. I found myself softly drawn into this unexpected final military duty.

After all, some months of study or reflection, thoughts of how to make a necessary fortune would now be welcomed. I had begun to love books and, though my taste of Europe had so far been severely flavored by the agonies of din and death with only the occasional if sparse consolations of Fléville and Mademoiselle Liliane, for now a term in England could even enrich my story. That enrichment, after all, was what was needed for the retrieval of the Louisville moment and the prize of lasting happiness which I knew was my due or at least my promise.

"What would you suggest yourself, Cranby?"

"I should take Oxford, major, if I were you?"

"May I ask why?"

"It has a ring to it. Oxford! Oggsford, you might say," he added with a laugh. "Not to be confused, of course, with our own Oxford in Lafayette County, Mississippi, a mere copy of the immortal original in England. This is the Oxford of all Oxfords, major. The grandsire of Oxfords. The name will resound forever in your life. Oxford – the one and only. If you are from there, they say, you will be welcomed anywhere."

We laughed together, as I had also laughed in the mud and gunfire with men like myself who came from nowhere to do battle, were wounded or killed and then dispersed to nowhere once again or – as I was now – to the new chapter of our lives. Most went home. That was no choice that I could take. I had things to do – a self to make.

"What are the formalities?" I asked Nick Cranby.

"It's your own free choice of university," he said, flicking through pages on his desk. "If you choose Oxford, you should also choose one of the colleges from among those who endorse the offer for American ex-military. They've also suffered a lot of financial hardship during the war, really hard, and I believe this gives them a bit of help from the government."

"But I don't understand," I said. "You mean, there is an Oxford College and then, within that college, there are – what? – other colleges?"

"Oxford, England, is a university. It's made up of independent units, or colleges, which decide for themselves who their students should be. And you would live in one of these so-called colleges as part of the university."

"And so – how do I choose from one of these... one of these colleges?"

"Not all have signed up for President Wilson's offer, though several have. Again, major, it seems you can take your pick."

"On what basis?"

"I have pictures – and notes of the college heads..."

Among his pile of papers Cranby had an assembly of sketches, photographs and letters.

"Here's one," he said, passing me a handwritten letter with a crest of what looked like three beheaded dragons in blue and gold.

It was signed *The President, Trinity College, Oxford*. The signature I made out to be Herbert Blakiston. The letter stated that the college would welcome men of excellence from the forces of the United States of America who had seen service with distinction in the Great War. Their fees and accommodation would be supported by the War Office. One or two fellows might also be supportive and their residence would remain confidential. No record of their period at Trinity would be kept in the college files, so that any of "our American friends and guests" who took up the offer would feel permanently safe from the inquisitive scrutiny of the newspapers of Fleet Street or any other prying intruders.

The note added, as I recall: "More than eight hundred of our own men from Trinity have served in the Great War and we therefore value the courage and sacrifice of our American cousins. We have had Americans studying with us before and they appear, with their loyalty, to have enjoyed the experience. Mr. Crosby, an American citizen, may also be tutoring here for a time."

"It sounds fine, "I said, "but who are these poor *fellows* who "might be supportive"? Are they the college servants maybe, the staff and the cleaners, the gardeners, shoe blacks?"

Cranby had clearly done his homework. He explained that "a fellow" was a distinguished member of the college and that the fellows, together, deliberated on issues of importance and policy such as the admission of courtesy undergraduates from abroad.

"There's also a bursary, major, or scholarship if you like. It's to do with the new IIE – the Institute of International Education, Butler-Root-Duggan some call it. Something over a hundred dollars a month."

Since the end of battle, and with the uncertainties as to how my necessary fortune was to be made, the prospect of new discoveries in Oxford, England, was something I chose no longer to resist. It could even bring me closer to her own world, as yet unreachable.

In a final gesture the diligent Cranby gave me a brief note about my college of choice.

I read that the college had once been called Durham College, a place for Benedictine monks and novice students. It became Trinity in March 1555, the year of Hawkins and the slaves of Virginia, and it was named for the citation as *The College of the Holy and Undivided Trinity in the University of Oxford, of the Foundation of Thomas Pope*.

Theology had been the main or even the sole study, and my imagination was quickened by memories of Louisville and of the Great War and that I had also, very briefly, been at the St Olaf's Lutheran College in southern Minnesota. All this let me lightly conjecture my time to come in Oxford, England, and in the sacred cloisters of Trinity College, as a robed and shaven-headed monk, sober and prayerful, rising before the light of dawn to intone the monastic chants that the Fellows of Trinity deemed appropriate for American soldiers, saved by their Lord from foreign graves.

I guessed that some who had known me would even, if in jocularity, say that there had always been something of the monk about me. It is true that, though a keen enough sportsman, I had not kept many close friends from my early years. In fact, reflecting on my earlier years, I formed the impression that my time at Trinity College, Oxford, would somehow make them irrelevant. My past, I suspected, would disconnect from my present. I would, in my own way, be an Oxford man.

The time was not long, a few weeks only, between my conversation with Cranby in Whitehall Street, Manhattan, and my arrival at what I later learned was called the Porters' Lodge at Trinity College.

There were hostels for demobilized soldiers in New York and, anticipating my monkish existence in Oxford, I spent a few last days walking the streets of Manhattan, fixing its aura and views deeply into my mind. I wore my uniform.

I am a patriot of what I hope is the better sort. I do believe that I would have died for my country and our allies if the Great War had held that to be my destiny. I am open, however, to the welcome changes of influence which derive from others. Mademoiselle Liliane of Fléville was illustrative of this. On the few brief occasions that I was away from the thrust of war, the days in Fléville reminded me of the equilibrium which men, at best, can find with women and their boast of life.

She was older than me and had that beauty which cannot be divided from the falls of nature: sun and fresh air, food from the land, songs in the natural harmony of life, and the latency of confidence that all women are right to claim but which too often is denied them through masculine fear and jealousy.

Fléville had been occupied by the Germans. An approximate report on what we did there came to my hands later. It read:

At 05:30 on the morning of October 4th, 1918, the 3rd Battalion, 16th Infantry Regiment, First Infantry Division, spearheaded the attack to liberate Fléville. It consisted of 20 officers and 800 enlisted men. After the battle, that evening, there were only 8 officers and 220 enlisted men left. The 3rd Battalion alone lost 12 officers and 580 enlisted men that day in heavy fighting against the Germans occupying Fléville.

I was almost captured. Without the aid of Mademoiselle Liliane I certainly would have been and may even have been executed. She had given me a German uniform which I was able to wear for several days and which enabled me to ascertain the German positions at a very local level. Later I was often teased that I "made a good German" and that I "could well have been a member of the family of the Kaiser himself". The man whose uniform I wore had died. It was even rumored that I had killed him. I had not. He died from nephritis, common enough in the war, fatal if untreated.

Mademoiselle Liliane and I were never lovers – or anything like it. Yet in the few days I spent in the village, close to the killing ground, I learned from her something like the reinforcement of intention. She was devoted to a young man who was also fighting, but far away, and was rumored to have been taken prisoner. She and I spoke together after the fighting was over and I stayed a while in Fléville. Her dedication reminded me of my own firm, one-second enchantment in the roadster at Louisville, followed by the shared glow, inward and out, at the fireside. Like her I could never lose that moment of miracle, that flushed second, when a person, man or woman, defines the course and justification of a life. Her man was called Jacques. The young woman who had changed everything for me was in Louisville, America – mine forever I thought, unknowing then.

Considering the events and losses of the past four years, albeit in distant Europe, New York was looking fine. I strolled at leisure, somewhat poor, often hungry.

Thinking perhaps that even a few hours of casual work might give me a handful of dollars to spend unwisely before

I sailed for England I chanced to pass Windbrenner's poolroom on Forty-Third Street, and went in to enquire whether they could use an extra attendant. There was nothing.

"You look hungry." A small man with a flat nose, a large head, tiny eyes, and conspicuous hair in his nostrils caught my arm at the door.

"You're a soldier, right? Well, you're in uniform so I guess that isn't great detection. We owe you things, buddy, let me buy you food."

He introduced himself as Meyer Wolfshiem and he gave me a generous lunch with a diluted wine he informed me was legal. At first he had suggested for our lunch Delmonico's on 44th and 5th Avenue but I asked him for somewhere less grand, more simple. We found a quiet place and table and with a sly look he ordered a wine by name.

"Diluted," he said, pouring water into the glass with the wine. "I wanna get used to it. Less than two point seven percent alcohol. The eighteenth amendment has not yet been passed. There's still the Wartime Prohibition Act. But we're OK. This is special. It's an Inglenook wine from California – won nineteen gold medals at the opening of the Panama Canal! Your good health, soldier!"

Even as I sat with him, tasting this extraordinary new child of the American harvest, I felt that some of the rhythms of my necessary and future life-to-be were taking shape. The meal must have cost him a fortune, and I was not sure of his hospitality till he asked me, over coffee, about my own life.

As it was so prominent in my mind it came out abruptly.

"Any day now I shall be going to Oxford, England. You know? I shall be studying at the famous Trinity College."

"Oggsford!" He said the word with a relish and a volume which attracted the waiters' attentions.

"You're an Oggsford man? Just what I'm looking for! You're a fine-appearing, gentlemanly young man, and you're going to Oggsford! I know I can use you good – if you're interested."

He explained, leaning forward across the table with something like a whisper that, with the ending of the war and the submission of Germany, there were great fortunes to be made by selling bonds which were now discreetly entering the markets from former German industries, in conjunction with anonymous partners in the United States of America. Together, in the hands of the right people, these could make comfortable millionaires of a chosen few.

"I seek a young unknown, a gentlemanly guy, with a sound manner and European connections, preferably ex-military and with a hero's record–to liaise behind the scenes as the flow of bonds amplifies and hits the markets in the–shall we say? – the more private corners of dealing."

I looked hard at him as would anyone with the ambitions I had stored away in my brain, those wild intentions to fulfill the promise of the Louisville roadster, the wealth I had seen and savored in her house, and the wealth required to concretize a dream. I looked hard at him because this man, this two hour-long stranger-made-friend, could be a fraud, a liar or a trap.

"It sounds very tempting," I told him with caution. "Unfortunately I have already received my acceptance, and a scholarship, for Trinity College in Oxford. My inclination is to spend some time there to meet new people. Learn a little. Ease myself from the war."

"Exactly! That is precisely what you must do! An Oggsford man is just what we need! You may have a companion in arms there too – if my colleague Borson Slagle has kept his word. But all that's for later – for the future, plenny of time. Do I have your hand?"

He put his right hand across the table and I could not fail to notice that his cuff buttons had been made from chicken beaks.

I hesitated. To express in full the state of mind of those of us who had fought, seen death, been near to death themselves, seen also, worst of all perhaps, good friends and colleagues die in blood and mud and in the kind of agony which simply does not exist in the lives or even the imaginations of those who have not been close, to try to express this in full, as it was for me in those days in New York and before Oxford, is impossible. It is impossible for the simple reason that events, in their recall, are not merely verbal but picture-shows in the brain, old movies, sounds beyond description, a whole sensory cavalcade which no dictionary provision can capture. And yet.

For me it was as if night had not, after all, fallen.

In France, in battle, we anticipated not merely sunset but the closure of all light and life – if not today, tomorrow. If not then, then sometime with the certainty of a setting sun into a near night from which we would never waken. Spared from death, I was free to manufacture myself and my deeds. So I took his hand. He squeezed mine warmly.

"You can trust me. Do I call you... Jay?"

"Gatsby. Gatsby's fine." I had changed my name at the age of seventeen, conscious then, if only slightly, that life was for my manufacture. Even the military, to my surprise and pleasure, officially accepted that I was no longer Jimmy Gatz.

"You can trust me," he repeated. "There are fortunes to be made. If we spread and diversify enough, and I know we can, tens of millions of dollars will pass to those who have had the foresight and the skill to make them their own. There's nothing crooked here, Mr. Gatsby, not a bit. It's a plain matter of being ready, having vision. There is, y'see, what they call "an unprecedented bull market". Take just one – Mercantile Marine – rising like crazy from under a hundred to over a thousand. I see you like my cuff buttons."

I may have nodded. I said nothing.

"I'm experimenting," he said, flicking the cuffs with something like pride.

"You can trust me," he repeated a third time. "Finish the wine. To the glories of America!" He raised his glass. I copied him. "By the end of this century we shall be the major wine makers of the world. I can see you want proof."

"Proof?" Incredibly I sensed that I did indeed trust this man.

The mental turmoil I have tried to describe enforced a kind of seizure of rescue. I was not a drowning man, nothing of the sort, and yet there was something within, some irresistible urge, which allowed me to reach out with confidence to something close and promised which would sustain me. Here, now, that something was the promises and person of Mr. Meyer Wolfshiem.

"You want proof?" he smiled. "Bide your time – but mark this:

"Later this year, October Second to be precise, there's the World Series. I can tell ya now what's goin' to happen. It'll be the Chicago White Sox and the Cincinnati Reds – if I'm not mistaken. The White Sox'll lose. There'll have been a lot of gambling and speculation, and fortunes'll have been made on that result. Some of the White Sox players'll probably be accused of deliberately losing. That it was fixed. No matter. Big fortunes will have been made. They'll be rewarded.

"I tell you this, Mr. Gatsby, only so's you'll know that you can trust me: if these occurrences don't occur, well, pull out from our deal at any time. I'm just a phony. But if I'm right, trust me, and with your gentlemanly skills you'll make a fortune."

He gave me contact information and a card. He said also that I would be contacted in Oxford – "but the fun really starts when you're home and able to travel – Chicago, Philadelphia, likely California. And here in New York close to Wall Street, of course, maybe the outdoor market in Broad Street."

We shook hands once more. He called one of the new Yellow Taxicabs, waved a last time, and I walked to Central Park, full stomached for the first time in many months.

I stayed in Central Park for three days and two nights. The days were not exactly radiant with warming sun but they were not too cold either, thanks to the uniform I wore. Nights in Central Park, as many can tell, are a magic of their own. On clear nights, and mine were clear nights, there, in the thick of one of the world's most fast-growing human collectives, you can see skies with stars whose number and vigor overwhelm the senses. Sometimes, and I was lucky, there is also the moon. It was a waning moon those couple of nights, gibbous in shape but as bright as a military buckle.

I woke one time in the night and it seemed like I was there, in the silvered dark, with her.

There is a speaking of looks that overrides and triumphs over language. I have mentioned more than once the white roadster moment in Louisville and what followed to unite us. In uniform then too, but a mere lieutenant, I had seen, or rather heard, the cheers of decades to come in her eyes. One of my certainties for Trinity College in Oxford was that I would have the time and the opportunity to shape the life and ownerships I needed for her. There, on that night in Central Park in my own internal picture house, I had walked from the dark monks' cloisters of Trinity College to where she was waiting in the Oxford meadow to join me in an eternity we both knew was our compulsion.

My life's incidents till then had signposted the road to the young woman I loved and who was mine, and also to the wealth which I now rejoiced would be mine through the agencies of Meyer Wolfshiem.

I had invented an altogether different story for my life and for my past, tailored for Trinity College, Oxford, and for any others who require status of anyone they could wish to befriend.

My own, true story, however, was different.

I have heard it said that when I was younger I was dismissive or even contemptuous of women. Those who judge rapidly and superficially have accordingly judged me to suit their own limitations. In women, as with Mademoiselle Liliane, I have always found a human harbor for the specialized emotions of modesty. By this I mean that with men, men including myself, the need is to prove and to combat – or so we have been taught. Modesty for most men is to be despised. With women it is possible for a man to be a truer self. This I found in France, and in that one sharp and etching moment in Louisville. Others would say that I knew women early. This is true. I knew, early, that women and one woman in particular, would define my entire life and fate.

At seventeen I had had a kind of confidence which owed nothing to my circumstances and all to my conjectures. My family was relatively poor. They worked the land but did not reap enormous reward. They lived in North Dakota. Still young I travelled through the neighboring states of Minnesota (where I had studied in a Lutheran college for a short unsatisfactory term), Wisconsin, Michigan, working from time to time at anything that came to hand: farm work, fishing, or occasional repair work.

For one full year I lived by Lake Superior and managed to make an existence by digging for clams and fishing for lobsters. It was there that I saw the yacht.

As in New York with the thoughts of Trinity College in Oxford, England, the yacht had made firm my fluid conjectures. These are often called milestones or turning points in our lives. For me it was something even stronger: Dan Cody, Meyer Wolfshiem and Trinity College were reconstituting surgeons who put together a man called Gatsby for the girl I loved, unaware of the cruel pain to come.

When I first went on the prowl at Lake Superior I was James Gatz, Jimmy, sometimes Jim, son of Henry Conrad Gatz of North Dakota, and his wife Yelena who died young, died when Jimmy Gatz was only eleven years old. Young Jimmy had been a planner, as later was Jay Gatsby.

As a child I used to detail my own daily timetable: my physical activities, my studies, my sport, and my curiosity about inventions and discoveries. I prescribed baths for myself as well as savings of cash (three dollars a week) and a respect for my parents. My mother was dear to me – more perhaps than I can now say or even fully recall. Her death delved a cavity of loss which perhaps nothing to follow could ever replenish.

At Lake Superior Jimmy Gatz, in torn and worn green jersey, with a thinning pair of canvas pants and twisted shoes, became forever Gatsby. It had been the sighting of the yacht *Tuolomee*, the property of Dan Cody, which conjured the metamorphosis.

I had borrowed a rowboat and shouted up to Cody that an imminent wind could destroy his vessel. Maybe he had pity, maybe he saw the mirror of himself, younger, when he made his millions from Nevada and the Yukon. Whatever the cause, he took me in.

I learned what it was to be rich, but rich for purpose. We also travelled, crossing seas to distant shores, and any sense of confinement I had acquired in North Dakota – where Fargo and the Pence Automobile Company were the heights of most ambition – was teased out forever through our voyages to the West Indies and places such as Praia on the island of Santiago in Cape Verde on the way to what Dan called the Barbary Coast.

I even danced there, once only and not well, a dance they called the *coladeira* with a girl of sun-lashed beauty called Mayra. I was not to dance again till later, till I was with Trinity College in Oxford, or rather at a club in London – and also at a spires and jazz celebration and a palace ball. No decent performance of the exotic *coladeira* then of course, however well I tried – but I had learned the foxtrot and was forced into my own terrible versions of the Charleston.

Meanwhile Dan Cody had already provided me with a costume fitting for the new character I was creating, that had been in Duluth before we sailed. He got me a fine and expensive blue coat, several pairs of white pants and a sailor's cap. Gatsby, Gatsby now, I thought, and forever!

The Great War clinched it: Major Gatsby, hero and medalist.

Thanks to European academic generosity and the amenability of our heads of state, I was to become a part of the most famed learning institution in the world: Oxford, England. Of all places too, that same Trinity College, cloistered and monkish no doubt but, as I was told, where Isaac Newton had seen his apples fall and changed the world forever with his gravity.

I returned for a last time to the hostel in Manhattan. There was a message for me from the conscientious Cranby: Please call in, major. Good news.

The Institute of International Education, supported by the well-disposed in England, were advancing me several hundred dollars as part of a scholarship and to enable my travel and settling to be comfortable.

I sailed from New York. Before embarking I gave a last call to Meyer Wolfshiem. He wished me Bang Vowidge and said Mr. Borson Slagle would likely contact me in Oxford, but to have a fine time, make contacts with the ambitious and the greedy, not to fall too much in love with the fast English girls, many now with lipsticks and cigarettes, and not to forget the World Series and his own prophetics. He said, yet again, that I could trust him. He proved to be right.

I sailed from New York on the *SS Bardic* of the White Star Line, setting foot in England for the first time in Liverpool. On the journey to England I had much time for reflection, reflections centered, especially on deck at night against the stars, on my future and my marriage.

It was my habit from childhood to write notes to myself, and these help in the telling of this story. Few of the passengers on the *Bardic* introduced themselves to me and likewise I seldom made myself known to others, preferring, as was becoming my custom, to remain detached from the throng, delightful though I found the bustle of happy or celebrating people.

One man I do remember was a genial Englishman who had also fought in the Great War and, more interestingly, had entertained the serving military at a place called Wimereux in the Pas de Calais. He was now hoping to be in a Broadway show which, he said, could sometime ahead open in London. His name was Stan Holloway and with a wink and a smile he said he was on his way to Hollywood.

"What sort of work do you do?" I asked him.

"Well. They call it concert parties. You get a lot of folk together, they dress up nicely, you see they get a bit to drink and something to eat – let 'em chat and have a laugh, the more the merrier – and then you do whatever you think best. They love you for it. Mark my words: anybody'll love you for it. Give it a try, mate!" He laughed and smacked my back.

In Liverpool, I stayed only one night at a small hotel close to the station of the London and North Western Railway. It was a cramped room with a narrow bed and what the proprietor called a chamber pot. The window view was restricted to the back of the station and a large poster for *Rowntree's High Class Chocolates and Cocoa*. It dominated the scene. I would never forget it nor the unavoidable role of advertisement in industrial landscape.

My chief recollection of the people of the town was of their immediate hospitality, their generosity. I went into bars which they called pubs and, though no longer in my uniform, my accent somehow stimulated their interest and they insisted on buying me drinks and offered foods which I did not recognize or choose to sample.

Unfortunately they sometimes had difficulty in understanding what I wished to say and I have to confess that when I had first set foot in Liverpool I assumed that those I met were speakers of native Irish or Scandinavians.

A similar problem of language arose when, on the following day, I managed to get a train to Euston Station in London, despite the news of strikes. Going first to London had been my own choice as the journey directly to Oxford from Liverpool was a very complicated affair and I wished, in any case, to see something of England's capital city.

At Euston, a porter as I guessed, came eagerly to help me with my very meager luggage and spoke in a tongue which I assumed at once to be Dutch.

When I asked him to speak English he said something which I afterwards took care to note in writing and which resembled, "Curb lie me gavna" and which made no sense to me at all.

Not to give offense I shook his hand and he appeared to stare at his palm with disbelief as I went off to seek the ways and means to travel on to Oxford.

Once again, thanks to the diligence of Cranby, I had an arrangement to stay for three nights at a hostel for ex-soldiers at an address off a street called The Strand in the vicinity of the attractive sounding Covent Garden. Until now, as we have seen, my European experience was confined to the battlefields and villages of France, and even in America I had only slight knowledge of the larger cities including New York

The hostel was called *The Sentinel* and thankfully the staff spoke in accents which to my American ears were at last intelligible. I shall never forget the kind, plump, shining doorman, Bert, who also took my particulars from behind the desk and guided me to my spotless if narrow bedroom from which I could just see the River Thames.

"'Fie can 'elp in any way at all, colonel," he said, willfully, I suspect, mistaking my rank, "jus' let me know."

I love jazz, I said.

"Y'mean music, sir?"

"Well, yes."

"Try the Prince's Theatre, sir. You'll get tickets if you show 'em this card. And I think you'll love the songs and that."

He gave me a small card with my name and an official stamp. I had the blue coat still that Dan Cody had bought for me in Duluth but, anticipating later needs, I asked Bert where I might find good pants – or trousers as they called them here.

"You'll find shops along The Strand, colonel. Good 'uns too. And don't forget to show' em the card I gave you. They'll see from that as you're a Yankee and as you fought with our Tommies in the war. They'll want to show respect to ya. Give ya good and honest prices. And if you've time look in the park for a bit, the Serpentine, see the swans – it's relaxing. Oh, and can I suggest you go to tuck in at the Lyons that's open opposite Charing Cross Station? They've got cakes, and cream, and apple pies like we haven't seen in London for the past five years. You'll love 'em."

I followed his advice, taking my time along The Strand to see what there was to see.

Gatsby, after all, would need what some people were calling sophistication.

Chapter 2

My impression was that, unsurprisingly, the people of London had been more affected by the Great War than had the people in New York.

There were signs of an understandable neglect in the way the sidewalks were cracked and unrepaired. The roadway itself was marred with small craters and unmoved dry patches of horse dung, though most of the vehicles were motor-driven. One or two of the shops had been repainted – I guessed in the spirit of a new world of peace and plenty.

The Strand itself was loud with noise. Public omnibuses weaved and turned to make their way through the tight traffic. There were even one or two surviving steam buses. On street corners small boys waved newspapers and shouted headlines. There were private motors too and most of these were of American design or origin. Older men, in bits of old uniforms from an even earlier war, stood at corners selling matches from trays strapped around their shoulders. One woman sang while nobody paid attention.

The people, who strolled rather more than the faster walking New Yorkers, appeared at my first sight to belong almost to two, or even three, different ages.

While most of those on the sidewalks of The Strand were pretty well like their counterparts in Manhattan – suits, shirts and ties of a standard sort – a few of the men, chiefly the older men, wore tall black hats or bowlers, one or two fedoras ahead of their time and even dark coats with tails. They were bearded too, some of them, though carefully trimmed and groomed and, as I passed close, I thought that a couple of these distinguished gentlemen were even scented.

Younger men, younger than myself, too young perhaps to have fought, were determined to be of a different age: blazers, flannels, old school ties with crisp cream shirts, maybe a straw hat, maybe a cane, no chance of a beard, maybe a moustache, sometimes a monocle, bright shining shoes, no inhibition when they followed the passing girls with their eyes.

The girls – no, the women – no, the ladies – were equally diverse.

To my American eyes, especially for whatever remained in me of North Dakota, some of these more mature ladies even went to extremes – extremes of elegance that is. Hugh hats, parasols (it was not raining), skirts made with enormous folds and flourishes of dazzling or demure materials especially silks. They had fine laces close to their throats with generally a brooch, jeweled or cameo, to adorn the neck. They had only the lightest powder on their cheeks if any, and held that faraway unconnected look which may denote confidence or extreme shyness.

Among them were, again, a younger set – as they were soon to be repeatedly called by the press.

Inevitably they vividly brought my love to mind: her dress, her aura, her speech, her movement, her gaiety – and her name.

Women the same age as Daisy, as Daisy Fay.

I had walked with her once in moonlight when we had kissed, then we had sat so close by that memorable fire – and she had looked so young and expectant with hope and certainty. We had also sat together in that white roadster and it had been as if our vows were made that instant.

Now along The Strand they walked, these girls, mainly in pairs, in shortened skirts, tight fitting hats – to be called *cloches* in the months that followed – long streaming strings of decorative stones around their necks and falling to their waists, powder, rouge and lipstick, and one young woman provoked a passing matronly dame to say aloud;

"How dare you!"

The girl in question shimmered in a frilled frock of shining pink. The heels of her strapped shoes were high, her silk stockings pale peach and gleaming, her cloche hat a dazzling white, small earrings of what may have been rubies were barely visible but, most noticeably of all, a burning cigarette in its elegant and very long black-and-gold holder was toyed with as a plaything, almost certainly more to shock than to enjoy.

There were two worlds here or even more, I concluded, seeing a young boy and a young girl, no more than nine years old, crouching and begging at one of the street corners, dirty and bruised, the boy with one eye missing, the girl in a woman's straw hat with decayed flowers and a filthy net:

"Spare a penny, mister." I put a shilling into the boy's held-out cap.

The English have often framed themselves as Victorians and Edwardians. We, in America, sometimes use the terms as a kind of shorthand. But here they could well describe how certain men and certain women were still to think of themselves, while others decidedly not.

Before my eyes I could see an England of reserve, of something of what I would perhaps later learn from Oxford, the "stiff upper lip" as I had heard it called. Before Trinity, that day watching the crowds in The Strand, my prophesies of Trinity were shaking and all too ready to be dashed. Pomp and circumstance? Maybe. Maybe not.

Checking later I found that it was Shakespeare himself who had designated pomp and circumstance in his play *Othello*:

Farewell the neighing steed and the shrill trump,
The spirit-stirring drum, th'ear-piercing fife,
The royal banner, and all quality,
Pride, pomp, and circumstance of glorious war!

Earlier in the century, as I also learned, the composer Edward Elgar was to use the phrase as a summary and banner for a defining part of the English self. As I observed the English, these notions seemed significant. How was I to know that later these things, this man, would come so close?

Did the young woman of The Strand indicate a closure to this spell of faith, this pomp and circumstance?

I hoped not. Deeply within, I was finding my own desire for show and pageant.

I found a promising-looking tailor's only a short walk from the hostel. Over the narrow shop-front it read: *Hartnell and Capaldi – Bespoke Tailors est. 1837.*

The moment I entered, a small white-haired cheerful and pink-faced man behind the counter, in caricature waistcoat, gold watch-chain, with a tape-measure, and spectacles on a silk cord balanced on his nose, eyed me up professionally from head to foot and with a wide smile asked me what he could do for me.

"I'd like to have some good quality pants," I said.

"Yes, sir. I understand that you are from the United States of America, would I be right, sir? You have lost a bit of weight recently, I should say, but I do already have a very fine pair of the best woolen pants – or trousers – which, with a little adjustment, would fit you to perfection, Would that be of interest, sir?"

"Sounds perfect!"

I tried on the pants which felt magnificent: best Scottish weave, he told me, very best wool and natural dyes, tailored by himself for a member of the royal family who, unfortunately, had changed his mind as to the color. To me they were a wonderful heather grey – if that makes sense.

He took my measurements and said: "they'll be ready for you in one hour, sir, with an extra charge of one guinea for adjustment, if that is all right with you, sir."

A guinea? A pig? Of course, no, it is one pound one shilling!

As I looked at my legs in the new pants in the long mirror I wondered what Daisy Fay would say to this English tailored elegance. Daisy Fay – and other girls too perhaps? No, just Daisy Fay!

Recalling as I write this the girl with whom I danced the *coladeira* in Praia, and Mademoiselle Liliane in Fléville, and the pretty waitress I was about to meet in the teashop opposite the Charing Cross Hotel in London, I struggle to define, to be precise, but can only say something like this: Daisy Fay was the summary or summation of them all. There was something of Daisy in all of them, but there was only Daisy in Daisy. Like a prisoner destined for a gilded cage, I was eager to begin, once rich enough and able, to serve my life sentence of joy with her alone.

"These pants are just what I need. Thank you. I'll be back in an hour or so."

I left the tailor's shop and walked west.

The girl was pretty, as I have said, and she smiled warmly when she asked me what sort of tea I would like and what sort of cakes or scones.

She wore a crisp black dress with a starched and stainless apron and one of those lacy head-piece caps with a black band of the sort I'd seen in the poster in Liverpool and later at Euston, selling *Rowntree's High Class Chocolates and Cocoa* with a smiling maid, two small children and a dog.

I knew nothing of teas or English scones so I asked her to bring whatever she thought would be right "for a visiting stranger".

"You're American?" she said.

"Right."

"I guess you might have been a soldier?"

"Right again."

"On your way home?"

"Just came to England. To stay for a while."

"On your own?"

"Guess so."

She brought me a homely tray with cup, saucer, tea-pot of china and a matching jug of milk. There were pieces of cake and buttered scones on a side plate.

"Why the milk?"

"Don't you take milk?" she asked me.

"Does anyone?"

"You really *are* American, aren't you?" She giggled and disappeared with the milk jug returning with hot water.

"Pour this in when you're ready. It'll still brew."

I did as she suggested. She stood alongside to watch me.

"My name's Beatrice," she said. "Though they call me Binnie. Binnie Hale."

"I'm Jay," I said.

"J for Joshua?"

"Just Jay – J, A, Y."

"Pleased to meet you, Jay," she said with a charming and open smile.

"Pleased to meet you too," I said, rising a little from my seat, half-believing this might be the custom.

"I don't want to sound forward," she said. "But are you likely to be doing anything next Thursday?"

"Why do you ask?"

"My uncle Albert has given me two tickets for Ella Shields – you know, Burlington Bertie – but my fiancé, Billy, isn't back yet from his regiment. She was American too, you know, Ella Shields. You being American…"

In the best, the truest and most original meaning of the phrase, I was charmed.

Oh, you English!

I'd heard someone say that on the boat, with a laugh, to a fellow passenger. I did not say it now to the sweet girl in the maid's outfit but I could not but feel it – an arrow of affection and the gratitude to fellow-humanity – when I saw the frank light of friendship in her eyes, the hoping turn of her lips, the sheer gorgeousness of woman-at-ease.

"I would really love that," I said. "Truly. Unfortunately I shall have left long before then. I have to leave London. I've just come down from Liverpool, on my way onwards. So sorry."

She smiled again, and picked up my empty cup and saucer.

"I was born in Liverpool!" she said with delight. "If you come back," she said, "it would be lovely to see you if you're free. I may not be here, mind you, it's just for a while, I need the money, see? But they'll tell you where I am," she giggled again. "Or where I might be performing. I don't want to be forward." She blushed a little and flicked her head. "You helped to save all our lives." And she was gone, Binnie, Beatrice. So English, so fair, so open, I thought.

Bert at the hostel, *The Sentinel*, had advised the Prince's Theatre and he had also given me one of the unofficial cards that some firms and businesses had made for the ex-military, cards they encouraged you to show to people who liked the idea of reciprocating what they saw as a sacrifice on their behalf to those who had fought.

I collected the by-now-perfect pants, showing the card Bert had given me. The tailor smiled, "let's just call it a pound, captain, if that's all right."

I put the pants on in my hostel room, a perfect fit which made me laugh aloud. I added a cream shirt I seldom wore with a necktie I had brought with me from a New York store, silk and turquoise, and the fine jacket Dan had got for me at Lake Superior.

The theatre was a short walk from The Strand: across Trafalgar Square with its blackened, pigeon-smeared statue of Lord Horatio Nelson, partly boarded, part-postered, past a church called Saint Martin's in the Fields and then through Leicester Square to Shaftesbury Avenue and the Prince's Theatre.

Outside the theatre was the following announcement:

After four years of war and its attendant miseries, what does the British public care about an inconvenience so comparatively trifling as a mere railway strike? Certainly not enough to permit itself to be kept away from an event of such prime importance as the Gilbert and Sullivan revival at the Prince's Theatre, whither an enormous audience gravitated to welcome Mr. D'Oyly Carte's excellent company on its first visit to Central London.

They charged me nothing for the ticket.

"You'll have to share a box, sir, but the pleasure's ours. The seat in the box has been specially requested for gentlemen in your position, sir."

Even the program was free and I read that the performance was a revival of a musical play, or operetta, called *The Mikado.*

The box was at a first floor level, to the right of the stage, and already three people were sitting comfortably in it when I entered. Somewhat to my dismay they were in full evening dress: a man of distinguished age, no beard but a trimmed and thickly dropping moustache, silver hair carefully combed towards the back of his head, white bow tie, tails, and immaculate white gloves. There was something a little familiar about his features – perhaps, I thought, a resemblance to some movie star.

A woman, about the same age, I took to be his wife. Her broad hat was clearly handmade and hand-decorated with flowers and a veil which she wore up. A pleated lace bib, with tucks and trims, adorned her chest, windowed in a velvet gown of rich ruby, extravagantly full on the arms and skirt, and carefully drawn, as if for a portrait sitting, around the base of her upholstered chair.

The third person in the box was, I guessed, their daughter.

Somewhat to my surprise, sitting discreetly in the shadow behind the door of the box was a uniformed London policeman, or "bobby" as I heard them called.

I hesitated to take my seat, although the gentleman and his lady smiled at me cordially, and the young girl glanced at me for only a second before turning her attention to the musicians in the orchestra pit.

"I do beg your pardon, sir," I said awkwardly. "I do not mean to intrude in this way. The young lady at the box

31

office seemed to believe that it would be in order for me…
I do apologize, sir. Please forgive the intrusion."

The elderly gentleman waved a hand.

"You must have been a fighting officer, young man. We are only too pleased to share the box with people like yourself. In fact, it was my idea that someone in your position should join us here. What was your rank?"

"I was a major, sir."

"Well done! And by the sound of it from Canada, if I am not mistaken?"

"Actually, sir, I'm from the United States of America."

"Even better! Without you, well, who knows, we can't be sure we'd have pulled through. Take your seat, young man. You are very welcome. Very. May I know your name… Major…?

"Gatsby, sir. Jay Gatsby."

He shook my hand.

"We are delighted you could join us, Major Gatsby. I'm Arthur Balfour. This is my sister Alice. And the young lady there is, like yourself, a comparative stranger to me who was brought to my sister's attention by the headmistress of the North London Collegiate School, a Miss Sophie Bryant. The young lady's name is Stella and, I believe, she is prominent in the Senior Drama Society and writes splendidly herself."

I stood up involuntarily at once, shaken, and found myself standing to attention.

"Excuse me, sir. You mean… I mean… am I right in thinking that you are the… forgive me, sir, I should have known better… aren't you the Prime Minister, sir?"

He smiled. And repeated: "Was, was, was! But please relax with us, major. Sit with young Stella here, you may have ideas to share, and I know she will enjoy your company.

You know the works of Gilbert and Sullivan? Have you seen *The Mikado* by any chance?"

"I'm afraid not, sir."

"Well, major, you are in for an agreeable evening."

"Thank you, sir, madam... and Miss...?

"I have also ordered champagne for the interval, major, and I do hope that you will join us."

The orchestra played an overture. The lights were lowered. The curtain rose and if I remember clearly enough – as the darkness and circumstances were not conducive to my notebook – a number of male singers in Japanese dress who introduced the work with a song:

If you want to know who we are,
We are gentlemen of Japan,
On many a vase and jar,
On many a screen and fan,
We figure in lively paint,
Our attitude's queer and quaint...

It was a cheerful piece of work, though I have to confess, jazz-lover as I am, that the formal orchestration and the neo-classic style came across to me as somewhat old-fashioned and nineteenth century.

The audience too, on the whole, flipped my mind back to the pre-war days, with their formal evening dress and dignified bearing. I did notice however, with some pleasure and a sense of affinity, that one or two of the young men were wearing what could only be called dazzling suits and some of the young women with them had the hair bobs and dressy shimmers that had been disapproved by the matron in The Strand.

At the interval, marked on stage by a medley of the songs so far – and I particularly recall something about *He's going to marry Yum Yum* – the champagne arrived as Mr. Balfour had promised. He looked down at the audience below and leaned towards me confidentially.

"I don't know about you, major", he said, "but people are all too willing to think they know me when all they've heard are the rumors. I've heard there's a thing called *the Balfourian manner* – a kind of cold, detached superiority, which shuns the warmth and company of others. You can see for yourself how wrong they are. But be prepared, major!" He smiled warmly and added, "You may even one day find yourself the subject of gossip and guesswork, yes, even a straight and decent young American like yourself."

I spoke only briefly to the young girl at my side. She was, she told me, seventeen years old, still at school and very pleased to be invited to the theatre. She hoped, though it was difficult for young women, to train as a journalist or writer.

"Where do you go next, young man?" Balfour asked.

"I go to Oxford, sir. You could say I have been drafted," I laughed.

He turned with something like enthusiasm.

"Why, that is wonderful! From the battlefield to philosophy! And whose idea was this, do we know?"

"I was told the Prince of Wales was involved."

"Good man! Won the Military Cross you know, but Kitchener was nervous the Germans might catch him and then what, eh? So when do you go, and where?"

"I go straight from here, sir, and to Trinity College."

"Trinity! Well, major, I was at Trinity too, you know, but at what they call the other place – Trinity Cambridge."

"There are two?"

"Yes, indeed. But I know one or two people from the

Oxford place. A fine President they've got with Herbert Blakiston, loyal and hard-working if ever was, and I believe I've met Tommy Higham, the Dean. Classics man. What will you study?"

"I don't think that's decided, sir. I understand it's fairly free and easy…"

"Look into philosophy, Gatsby, that's my advice. That and literature. The years ahead are a total mystery, so look after the inner man, Gatsby, the inner man… here we are!"

The lights dimmed once more, the orchestra played, and soon in this second half I was delighted with the madrigal several of the cast sang together:

Brightly dawns our wedding day,
Joyous hour we give thee greeting,
Whither, whither art thou fleeting,
Fickle moment prithee stay
Fickle moment prithee stay.

Even then, even with the formality of the theatre, even with the Prime Minister-that-was of England, even with all this and the turmoil and muddle of the months, the words brought a hope and vision to my mind, even as the cast was singing, the words became, tritely, my own:

Brightly dawns our wedding day, oh Daisy Fay, oh Daisy Fay!

We would, I knew for certain, be together, always and forever, in a bright dawn of soon-to-come. I could not know that the fatal note at Trinity was yet to arrive.

The performance ended. The audience rose to its feet though we, in the box, police constable included, kept to our seats and the half-shadow.

"We shall have to wait till the theatre is empty, gentlemen," the constable told us.

"Of course, Jenkins. We can wait." He turned to the girl who had been silent, though conspicuously attentive, for most of the evening.

"You'll be going straight back home, I expect, Miss Gibbons? Back to Kentish Town? We have transport for you and my sister here will accompany you."

"Thank you, sir."

Mr. Balfour turned to me: "Miss Gibbons has shown signs of remarkable gifts and discipline, though I understand that her situation is not ideal for her ambition. This is why my sister has asked that she might accompany her from time to time to events of this kind: artistic, you might say, crafted, and, above all, professional."

I got the impression that Stella Gibbons, if that was her name, did not take too kindly to being discussed in this way in her own presence. She said nothing, preferring to study the audience as they made a line together to leave the theatre, the Edwardian-style grandees with a mix of the daring and colorful young.

It struck me, perhaps more than ever before, that the younger folk were bound to be something of a distorted mix, so many of the young men having been killed in the Great War. Looking down into the auditorium some of the young women, though still in their twenties, were accompanied by gaily dressed boys, some perhaps not even yet twenty-years old. This too, I thought, would add to the marked differences of style and fashion.

At last the theatre was empty and Mr. Balfour's sister Alice, with Miss Gibbons, was escorted to a waiting taxicab. For a moment, Constable Jenkins beside him, Mr. Balfour faced me without speaking.

"It has been my pleasure to share the evening with you,

Major Gatsby," he said. "I'd be grateful if you would keep our brief encounter to yourself. Not that I am not proud to be your host but gossip and tittle-tattle delight some of the sillier press and I like to keep my reputation as a detached and somewhat cold individual intact.

"When I was pressing for ideas such as a home-land for the Jewish people I found it helped to be regarded as unmoved by emotion or angered by injustice. I'm thankful to your fellow-countryman John Stoddart who had the same ideas. Get hold of his *Lectures* when you can. But put aside this time together, if you would, don't speak of it.

"I am not expecting you to forget our charming evening, Gatsby. I just do not wish you to speak of it to anyone."

He held out his hand.

"I predict a good future for you, major. After Oxford – and Trinity no less! – you will return home no doubt to teach and instruct, and your Trinity-gained wisdom will be of great value to the young. Goodbye, sir."

A motor drew up from the shadows. Constable Jenkins opened the door and Mr. Balfour climbed in, the policeman following. I saw a gloved hand wave as the vehicle passed. I waved too.

The night was cool but pleasant, the sky clear with its partial moon and, even against the street lights, a number of the bolder stars were visible.

I decided to walk, to walk and to give myself up to Daisy Fay. After a few enquiries of passers-by – who responded with a warmth and ease which I felt I had not found so common in New York – I strolled up to Oxford Street, crossed the Circus, and then along Hyde Park to Lancaster Gate. There I decided to enter the gardens and to see the Serpentine that Bert had mentioned at *The Sentinel*.

Close to – I think it was called Queensway – a woman stepped in front of me. She was probably quite young but her drawn, white and punished features made her look older. She was wearing a straw bonnet and a cloak.

"You on your own, duck?" There was no smile, no seeing, but she opened her cloak, turning from the roadway towards me, to show her naked, frail and shriveled breasts.

"I've a place down there. We could go there if you like," she said, covering herself and pointing vaguely across the road. "Only a guinea."

"Sorry," I said. "Sorry... I..."

I knew that I had half-crowns and florins in my pockets. Taking a clutch of them I gave them to the woman.

"Bless you, love," she said, counting the coins as she spoke. "Bless you, dear. Me hubby died at Passchendaele, see, and I still have the kiddy, our Joe, to feed and that. Bless you."

She crossed the road quickly and before long had disappeared. Another thought occurred as I watched her go.

I was meeting them, these women, and keeping the altar of Daisy Fay dressed and flowered for wedding time. What if, however, what if some radiantly authentic young girl, with one fresh look at me, one moment of magical encounter, could blot out my unwavering devotion? I allowed the thought its time of fair meditation, concluding once more there was no such radiant or authentic girl. Only Daisy Fay. Just her.

It was dark by now and the tall railings of the park, with no access to gates that I could find, compelled me, looking quickly to left and right, to climb over as smoothly and noiselessly as I could.

The place seemed empty. I distanced myself briskly from

the Bayswater Road and hoped that I'd reach the lake if I went further into the park. These were my thoughts, so often repeated.

Daisy Fay: she was a great comfort for me, as she had been in France through all the screams and terror, through the machine-guns' blasts which, finally, I myself had commanded. The comfort was that of indestructible certainty. Just as a watcher of the skies knows that the early glow to the horizon of the east is the inevitable prelude to the rising of the sun, so I also knew, through all those months, that Daisy and I were a force of destiny. Walking now in solitude through the dark evening of a London park I allowed my memory and mind to run and run again the thoughts of her. Rough-necked all-American boy I may have been, I was unashamed of what some might take for mediaeval chivalry, a pastoral romanticism, or poetic flare. I have mentioned the moon that night, and the stars, as I had also watched them in Central Park. From nights in France and from the insights of other men, I could make out the shape of the Plough and from that calculate the position of the North Star or Polaris and from there Ursa Minor.

There they were, and hundreds besides, less visible at the horizon and over the trees owing to the glow of London lights, but with them and their eternity this rough-neck all-American soldier was in the zone of permanence and love. She would no doubt now be readying herself to dance in Louisville under these same stars and this same moon, if hours later. They would bring to her mind her "Dearest Jay"–as she had named me in the letters I had received from time to time.

I had kept the letters of course. They were short and simple. Thanks to the United States concern for us fighting men that, whenever possible, even the troops at the front could get the letters posted to them from home, one or two even reached me in France. One, I recall now with some obvious pain, was handed to me as I was helping to lift the dead body of my friend Chuck Deacon from the muddy pit where he had lain for two days.

"Dearest Jay," it read, "I do not stop thinking of you and of the times we were together, especially the time in Louisville on that evening under the trees, remember?

"I miss you, my love, and people tell me that the war will soon be over. I do hope so. We shall be together forever, I know.

"I still wear the hat you liked so much. Naturally I think of you whenever I wear it, though I have changed the ribbon to a darker green. If you remember you said that was one of your favorite colors.

"I am yours, Jay Gatsby, always, and for our own sweet love, Daisy."

"Hey, you! Whatcha doin' 'ere this time o'night?"

The voice came from the shadows in the park. I could see no-one at first then I made out a bench by a pathway and someone slumping there.

"Who are ya?"

Curious, I walked up to the bench and found an elderly man sitting in the dark. He had the features to suggest dignity and even learning but was dressed in a way which compelled the description of hobo.

He patted the bench at his side, inviting me to sit. I did so. Surprises in my recent life had been enough to make this natural.

"Who are you and what are you doing?"

I noticed that his manner of speaking had changed and,

close to, it was more in keeping with his worn though still refined features, bringing to mind something I may have seen in the Metropolitan Museum of Art on Fifth Avenue, the bust of a statesman maybe, Greek or American, I can't be sure.

"I'm just visiting," I said. "I felt the need for a bit of solitude."

"You sound American."

"That's right."

"Where from?"

"Oh, I've been about," I said. "No roots now."

"Like me," he said. "My name's Olman." He held out a hand. I shook it. It was firm, strong even, but bony too and dry. "Anything special you're looking for?"

"I guess not. Just biding my time. I heard there's a good lake here – the Serpentine?"

"You're going to swim?"

"No, but I like water."

He pointed into the middle distance, away from the main road where I had climbed in.

"Easy enough to find," he said. "You see that green light at the end of that turning? That's the path down to the Serpentine bank. They turn it to red if there's a problem or danger. Just keep your eyes on the green gaslight there and you can't go wrong. But first, young man, I want to tell you something. You see, I too came here just to think, just to be on my own. Then I sort of made a wish that someone might turn up, someone special, maybe receptive. What's your name?"

"Jay. Jay Gatsby."

"You made that one up, I can tell. But it doesn't matter. Sounds more like a fictional character or the title of a book, or one of your new Hollywood films – Ernst Lubitsch, I read about him, you've got a bit of a look of him. No matter. I'll call you Jimmy if that's OK, suits you more."

"As you like – though the name's Gatsby, Jay Gatsby."

"I lost four sons in the war. Four. My wife only stayed with me because of the lads. She had what you might call social ambitions. Years back she had an affair with the Earl of Doncaster while he was still a young man. Before we married, mind you. But it gave her ideas. She wanted the fancy life of the rich and aristocratic. You and I both know that that's the road to destruction if ever there was one, eh? She wanted big parties, lots of people, fine clothes, champagne and all the latest dances. Well, look at me – an amateur mathematician and not a good one at that. So when the lads were killed, and we got the news, it wasn't long before she was off with Harvey Maelstrom, Sir Harvey, that is.

"But I don't want to talk about me, Jimmy. I want to talk about you.

"You see, I can tell by your hands and your manner that you've been fighting – no, no need to tell me! It's over now, Jimmy, and you've your life to make."

He stared out in silence for a long moment, then turned to me and cleared his throat.

"While I sat here waiting and knowing that someone would turn up, someone to take the place of one or other of my sons, I had a vision of what was going to happen. Let me tell you.

"They say that was the war to end all wars, and know something? – they're dead right! Wars are finished now once and for good.

"So a man like yourself has a whole life ahead of him, a life of peace and plenty. Use it, man, use it! What's your gift?"

"I don't understand."

I was uncomfortable now and the place, and this man, were almost as if in a dream. I was keen to leave him, to get away. It was, as we know, already fixed in my mind what ambition I had – as for gifts, I had no gift beyond the determination to find and remain forever with the woman I loved.

"You're going to do fine things, Jimmy, mark my words. At a guess, you've had a tough life so far, hard up as a child, hard work as a lad, and then the war. You're keen to get on, I can see that too. So educate yourself.

"Know something? About fifteen years ago we had a fellow over here from Princeton University. He came to talk about schools and education. His folk were from Scotland but you'll have heard of him for sure. I'm only telling you this because I can see in your face that you've got what it takes to do what he did. One day, Jimmy, you could be President of the United States of America. That's a fact!"

"You mean President Wilson, of course."

"Dead right! It could be your turn in twenty years time. You've got years and years of peace and progress. Work at it, son. What did you say your name was?"

"Gatsby."

"Never heard of it, but you will have your fun. All right then. President Gatsby, what? Think about it. Think about what you can do – I did once, and I thought I'd leave it to the lads to carry on. They were all killed, every last one of them. Don't be distracted. President Gatsby – the great Gatsby, eh? Just think about it. Remember you met me. Remember the time and the date. And the place: Kensington Gardens, London, England. Remember me when you walk into the White House, eh? Now, off you go.

Get yourself a motor boat when you can afford it. Speeding on water's good for excitement and push. I've said what I wanted to say and that's it. Think yourself great, Jimmy, great as in great. You can do it! Just don't be distracted by anything. How do you say it now?... so long, soldier!"

He seemed to disappear.

If it had been a dream, as it felt, that would have been the only explanation. He rose from the bench, though with a swifter and smoother movement than I could have thought possible. He may have swiveled and touched me on the head, a gentle touch, an uncle – but that might have been a breeze in the park or even a falling leaf. When I stood up myself, there was no sign of him. I shuddered.

Before me, in the deepening darkness, was the green light of the Serpentine. I walked towards it, and as I approached the light from the moon made glitters on the surface. Closer still, the moonlight focused to a path across the water. Then, suddenly, the waters were ruffled as someone swam towards the green light. I was now almost certain that the last minutes were a dream and still remained so. I stood still, at a short distance from the water, as the swimmer came to the edge nearest to me. Then she arose.

It was a woman, naked, white and gleaming in the moon glow. To my consternation and shock she did not climb from the lake but pulled herself alongside the path, easing herself half from the water, and revealing, or so it seemed from where I stood, that her lower body was that of scales and a tail, that she was, unbelievably, a mermaid or siren.

Fear took hold of me. I turned at once. Not wishing to be heard or noticed by this dreadful apparition I stepped carefully on to the grass and walked with a swift but padding fall as far as I could. At a distance, I turned once more:

there was the green light, and there, just visible, was the silver siren of the London park. I believe she sang – or else my frighted brain was whirling in distraction.

I have subsequently understood that I was hallucinating and not only then. This may have been the unknown effects of the battles and my loneliness. Worst of all, as I climbed out of the park, close to what I later understood to be the Albert Memorial, the thought occurred to me that the siren had the face of Daisy Fay, compelling the belief that no such thing had occurred. And Olman? I put him totally from my mind as well. I have only set down these incidents because I am aware they are unlikely to be read or seriously considered by anyone as my future unfurls and a better account of my life is there for the telling.

I found that I was now in a district called Knightsbridge and, asking the way once more, I was soon hurrying towards Piccadilly, from there to *The Sentinel* where I felt relief and comfort.

Bert was off duty now, it was later than his shift. But the young night porter told me there was a telegram for me.

I opened it in my room.

It read:

URGENT STOP GO TOMORROW TO CHANCERY LANE STOP FIND WALTER CHASE COMPANY STOP SIGN ALL THE PAPERS PRESENTED STOP DO NOT ASK QUESTIONS STOP KEEP THE PACKET HANDED TO YOU STOP SIGNED BORSON SLAGLE FOR WOLFSHIEM STOP

The next day I did as instructed.

The Walter Chase Company took some finding, a small plaque by a doorway in Chancery Lane. There appeared to be just one front office and a backroom on the third floor.

The man behind the desk, tall, thin, in shirtsleeves and waistcoat, with a gold watch-chain, a hanging gold sovereign, and a very firm and confident English accent, said simply:

"Major Gatsby?"

I nodded.

"The papers are all ready for transfer to America. I was told to inform you that the bonds are worth a great deal and will be invested in the first place in drug stores across the Union. Your signature, as an American citizen and former serving officer, means that I can transfer all of them quite legally. If, however, there are any formal enquiries I have also been told to tell you that you must inform the authorities that these bonds were a part of your inheritance. Is that understood, major?"

I signed the papers, several of them, and could not help noticing that sometimes, above the signature, were specified sums of around eighty thousand US dollars or fifty thousand British pounds. I asked no questions, as instructed. A thick package was given to me.

Leaving Chancery Lane, I walked for a while towards Holborn. I was, I confess, breathless – breathless and shaking a little. The feelings did not last as I reminded myself, almost with spoken words, that my American dream was to be realized, and that the trophy to be won, however long ahead, was Daisy Fay. Anything, anything at all, was justified.

In my room at the hostel, where the genial Bert greeted me with his great smile and a letter that had just arrived, I opened the packet I had been given at the Walter Chase Company. It contained five hundred British five-pound notes signed, I noticed, by cashier Harvey of the Bank of

England. Two thousand five hundred pounds. I already had the knack of quick conversion: almost four thousand American dollars.

The letter was from Daisy. It was several weeks old, having traveled from one of my addresses to another till, finally, London. It began "Dearest Jay..." and went on to confirm her undying and undiminished love. I counted the bank notes several times and could not prevent myself from laughing.

The future was sure. She would be mine.

Chapter 3

I arrived at a station in Oxford sometime in the afternoon. It had a good feel to it, I have to say, though the station itself was none too clean, the facilities few but the staff and the station-master helpful and courteously warm in the way I had begun to associate with the English.

There was a refreshment room where I ate a cake of a kind I did not recognize – thick and fruity, iced with a layer of jam and cream – and I drank, inevitably, tea into which, once again, milk had been poured. My bags were light, and I had the best part of four thousand American dollars in my luggage, more than enough to take care of anything I might require for months ahead.

"Do you know Trinity College, miss?" I asked the young woman in a floral pinafore who was clearing my table after I had eaten the cake and drunk the milk-spoiled tea.

"It's in the Broad Street," she said. "Not a long walk. If you can find the market and the corn market it's just off from there. You American?"

"That's right."

"You'll know Douglas Fairbanks then?"

"'Fraid not."

"Lon Chaney?"

I shook my head.

"Rudolph Valentino? If you're American you must know Rudolph Valentino."

"Haven't had the pleasure. Maybe one day," and I half meant it.

"You a country boy then?"

"A soldier."

She blushed.

"Of course! How silly of me. No charge for the tea and cake, mister. It's on me."

"You said – the corn market?"

"That'll get you to Trinity. Nice to meetcha." She disappeared behind the counter and was busy washing the plate and cups.

The first bits of Oxford struck me most of all by their ordinariness. Houses, none grand here like the Fays' house, but with shops here and there, small churches or chapels. There was the occasional horse and carriage and I saw in that short walk two or three of what I learned were called the Oxford Bullnose automobiles.

Already these looked historic. I had a liking for cars – not just for white roadsters with Daisy Fay in them – and I guessed these open-tourer two-seaters were already at least five years old, which is to say from before the Great War, and things were moving fast.

I learned with surprise that Oxford was a kind of center for the motor business in England and was to see one of those responsible. These Bullnose Oxfords I had never seen in the States. They looked cute, as Daisy would say. Not for Gatsby though.

The walk to the corn market, which I discovered on arrival was, in fact, a roadway called the Cornmarket, took me less than half an hour. I had passed a good sample of Oxford folk on the way.

You could easily tell the difference between the working men and women in their thick tweeds and jackets, rough shirts and scarves, "corduroys", hob-nailed boots, and those I took to be members of the college – no, the University – more formally dressed, even with gowns and those square hats that forced me to smile.

I now have something to confess.

Suddenly I decided, as we say, to quit.

From New York, or even Liverpool or London, the semi-fiction idea of being a student at Trinity College, of the University of Oxford, England, had all the fantasy enrapture of a fancy dress ball (of which, incidentally I had so far only heard and never participated).

I had imagined Trinity College, given the brief history I had been told, as a mediaeval and monkish institution, possibly sworn to vows of silence, with morning incantations in fusty and candle-lit chapels at four in the morning, shaven tonsured novices talking in whispers to me in Latin, hard cold mattresses, and possibly even symbolic lacerations before bed.

With what I had seen from the railway station, the Cornmarket and from there onwards – I had decided to explore a little – to St Giles Road, passing a hotel called *The Randolph* and a museum called *The Ashmolean*, with model T-Fords passing each other on the road, and finally pausing with my bag and my fedora at an inn called *The Eagle and the Child* for refreshment, this short excursion taught me that my preconceptions were distinctly in error. It was not what I had imagined.

Among the black-gowned and black-capped scholarly gentlemen, young men in more-or-less elegant suits strode the sidewalks. Young women in spectacles, wearing blue-stockings, and laden with tomes and files, gave me short and telling glances as they passed. (I had no idea what these glances could have meant – my hat perhaps?)

The sun shone on the trees and the stones of St Giles, and the host at *The Eagle and the Child* was perfect for any illustration for Frank Baum – a wizard in shining spectacles and ruby shirt with a yellow cravat and a magic cap with a tassel.

"Now what would you like me to get you, sir?"

"Is there anything you would particularly recommend?"

"Ha-ha. I hear, if I am not mistaken, that you are from the United States of America."

"That's right. Is it so obvious?"

"It is quite apparent, sir. But be proud! Your people have much to be proud of. Let me offer you a pint of our very special Brakspear Draught Bitter Beer, sir. Dates back to the year 1711 while your country and ours were still under the same monarch, sir – good Queen Anne. On the house, as we say. My bet is that you have been a soldier and fought alongside our own boys – some of whom, I am pleased to say, are already making their way back to their studies here in Oxford."

He pulled with a joyful and muscular energy a foaming pint of beer which he set before me on the bar counter.

"Where are you from, sir, if you don't mind my asking?"

The half-prepared answer, the made-up answer-for-Oxford (and the future) came out at once:

"San Francisco."

"Sounds Spanish to me, sir. But look, we have some pigs' fry and some meat puddings if you're hungry."

"I'm fine," I said, lifting the beer glass which was full to overflowing and making my way to a quiet corner. It was there, thinking alone for an hour or more, that I found I had much to confess – to myself. Perverse these thoughts may be, but I had to let them ride.

First, it would perhaps have been better if Daisy Fay

and I had agreed that whatever our love had once been, it was now over. The Great War had come between us. We were apart. She would, perhaps and likely, find herself in the rich and coaxing society that was hers, and I would be forgotten. How prophetic this distortion later proved to be!

Second, this Oxford was not the monastic place I had pictured. It was a lively and teeming modern city, with an automobile industry of its own, young and outward-looking men and women, returning fighters of more courage and endurance than myself, theatres, picture houses (I guessed), museums, jazz (I hoped), dancing and social challenges which, with my American poverty, would be likely to overwhelm me.

These, as I say, were among my thoughts for an hour or so. People came and went from the tables. I decided to relax and resign myself to reality: even to quit.

I had cigarettes in a case in my luggage bag: Philip Morris and the remainders of some tough-smoking French Gauloises. I did not smoke much but I decided to smoke now. I took out the cigarettes, decided on the American brand and put it to my lips. I had no matches.

At the next table, reaching over to me and passing me a new Ronson Wonderlite, a young man smiled brightly and said:

"Please try this, it's the latest thing."

"Thank you, sir." I lit the Philip Morris and handed back the device.

"Have you just arrived?" the young man said. "I mean the luggage..."

"An hour or so."

"Here to study?"

"I hope so," I said with a smile.

People had told me, now, then and long before, that my smile was something of a warmer. I can only plead that it was part of a spontaneity that I did not always have the confidence to display. Even now, with the young man at the near table, I found myself speaking with a curious and very recent fusion of English and American. It was as though my mouth was seeking a deliberation and poise of its own. I urged myself to desist at once.

"Which college, may I ask?"

"Well, Trinity, though I haven't…"

"Goodness. I'm a Trinity man too! Welcome! My name's Norrington – Arthur Norrington – though for complicated reasons they call me Thomas."

We shook hands.

"My name's Gatsby," I said. "Jay Gatsby. It's a great pleasure to meet my first Trinity man. You just arrived too?"

"No, been here a while. Look, sorry, but I have to rush off. I have an appointment with the Dean, Tommy Higham – something to say about Virgil, would you believe? Let us meet again later, any time. Sherry? You are truly welcome. Guess you were in the military, yes? Anyone who's served in the military deserves the welcome and respect of Oxford. As far as I'm concerned they'll always get it. 'Bye now."

We shook hands again and his openness and warmth dispelled some of the misgivings that my private thoughts had invoked.

Olman, the ghostly figure in Kensington Gardens, had told me to be steadfast, told me, in so many words, that I would win. My own instincts took the same direction.

Right then, steadfast I would remain!

Most of all, I would win! Daisy longed for me as I longed for her. Right! She was to be the centre of all things! I would reach wealth at whatever cost! I would, as I had already thought, manufacture my new self, my life, my position and my love.

Sitting in that Oxford inn, the sun soft on the leaves of St Giles, my own truth and my past floated away from me, the shores of the lake, the sailings around the Indies, the poverty and the embarrassment, the first relief of my lieutenant's uniform – at last, I could not be judged! By anyone!

Gatsby, Oxford, wealth, a palace in Louisville, and Daisy – og de levede lykkeligt til deres dages ende – an expression I loved.

I took another beer and returned to the table where Norrington had spoken with me. I thought hard – mused, some might say. Resolute as I was in my determination to make and shape my future after all, I confess to a certain misgiving, a fear almost, of what Oxford could hold.

These were Englishmen of huge confidence and history, and despite whatever I aimed to become, or whatever stories I were to spin about San Francisco and my grand tours of Europe before the war, the American in me carried, as for so many of us along with the strength of newness and energy, a shyness at the European feast. We were youngsters after all. Plato and Socrates, Dante and Shakespeare, Newton, Galileo, and Beethoven were all in the family tree of those I might soon be meeting.

So what? The voice inside me was loud, loud from the battlefields of France, from the shores of Lake Superior and from the magic of Manhattan. I'm an American! And we, and I, are the future!

I finished the beer and walked out into St Giles. It was still quite early in the year. The trees were budding or in leaf and the sun shone knowingly upon them. There was a college across the road from where I was walking towards the Cornmarket and I crossed, avoiding one or two horse-drawn carts, some Oxford Bullnoses, and the more prevalent Fords, with a whole battalion of bicycles.

There were both young men and young women on the cycles and, again, I was struck by their airs of confidence and belonging. I had much to learn from Oxford – not so much as to how I could make myself rich for Daisy Fay, as to how the new Gatsby could find a repose to accompany his quest and his status.

Let me be frank once again: I am, to the core, an American and proud of it. I knew my country had just saved Europe from an atrocity. I knew too that this would not be required ever again in the future. Wars are ended – at last! – but the United States would, for certain, be the grounding for youngsters like myself: eager with energy and trust, pioneers of courage and democracy, enablers for those with nothing but hope and intention – myself, the Gatsby: that which was bound to be.

I set this down here – for my country 'tis of thee – as a prelude to all that I was willing to ingest from Oxford. I had only met one fellow student – undergraduate – so far, comparable to myself and my own temporary status, but the man, Norrington, had the warm and easy openness that I was finding in so many of the English. Yes, I still quaked a little at how I was to assign myself. But the signs were good.

On the far side of St Giles I discovered that the glorious and aging stone belonged to St John's College. I nervously looked into the college, unsure of my rights or preventions.

"May I help you, sir?"

A genial and distinguished man in dark jacket, starched shirt, and bowler hat, was speaking to me through a window. At the same moment I heard a band strike up, somewhere within the college, jazz for heaven's sake! I recognized the tune too – it was Clarence Williams, piano and blues, Chicago and New York, and the song, the song, the song... yes, it was *Baby won't you please come home*.

I had heard it in France too, just a few months before, with Mademoiselle Liliane, at a break in the fighting, a weekend of recovery, and they were there to cheer the troops – or to make them melancholy for home:

Baby won't you please come home,
'Cos I'm here all alone.
Every hour in the day
You will hear me say
Baby won't you please come home, I mean
Baby won't you please come home.

"May I come in here, sir?" I said to the man at the porters' window.

"May I ask who you are, sir, and what is your business?

I held up my luggage bag.

"I just arrived from America," I said. "I'm to join Trinity College for a while. I guess you could say I am just getting my bearings. I heard the music. I love jazz."

"By all means, sir. It's some of the new undergraduates, and there's a young lady with them who sings. You'll find Mr. Turnbull in the dining hall, sir, a new fellow, he loves music. Normally his taste is for chamber music but he's very broad-minded and likes to encourage anyone with a flair you might say."

He pointed out the way for me to go, but I could simply have followed the sound. There was a fine piano, clarinet, bass, and – I wasn't sure – a few short trumpet bars perhaps. As I approached the door, a woman's voice, right on the beat, wonderfully rangy, clear as a bell on the words was singing:

I'm gonna telephone my baby
Ask him won't you please come home
'Cause when you're gone
I'm worried all day long
Baby won't you please come home
Baby won't you please come home.

When the music ended I stepped a little further inside and an older man came up to me with a broad smile.

"You must be Carl Summers," he said.

"I'm afraid not. My name's Gatsby. Jay Gatsby – I'm sorry if I've..."

"You are a friend of Carl Summers perhaps?"

"Sorry, sir. I don't believe I ever heard of him."

"We were expecting him. I believe he was coming down from Glasgow. One of the few tenors who can sing modern jazz and decent *lieder*. What brings you here then, Mr. Gatsby?"

"I just heard the music, sir, and the gentleman at the gate said I could come in."

"Of course! Of course!" He held out a hand. "I'm Herbert Turnbull, just become a Fellow of St John's. Teaching mathematics but also very keen to encourage the undergraduates to love music. You probably heard me playing the piano just now!"

To say that I was stunned is banal. Here was this thin, bespectacled, grave-looking English gentleman in his mid-thirties and a mathematician at that, whom I had just heard playing in a way of which Sidney Bechet or Mope

Desmond would not have been ashamed. My preconceptions, not for the first time, were taking another striking hit.

"You play, I take it, Mr. Gatsby?"

"I'm afraid not. I just love to see the dance... and to hear the jazz."

"And chamber music, *lieder*?"

"Not quite yet, I'm afraid, sir. Perhaps Trinity College will introduce me."

"You are at Trinity?"

"About to be."

"Well come and meet some of our wonderful players."

To my surprise, yet pleasure, he took my arm and led me into the hall where the young musicians were taking their break.

"This is Delmore, Richard Delmore, you will have heard him playing the double bass just now. And the young man with the clarinet is Thomas Ewan, while the fellow with the trumpet over there is Henry Vennick – though I think you are still determined to learn and practice, Vennick, isn't that correct?"

"Quite, sir," he said, his eyes brightening, then addressing me. "I was over in America some months ago. Great place! I had the good fortune to be taken by my hosts on a Mississippi River Cruise. It changed everything..." He looked shyly at Herbert Turnbull. "I mean, it gave me a wish to be able to play the trumpet – I mean the jazz trumpet."

"I envy you," I said politely.

"There was a very young man there with the band. He was, well, unforgettable. We talked and we shared a beer as the boat cruised the river," the young man's enthusiasm was infectious. "Idyllic, imagine: the sun, southern beer, and the magic of this new music. He was only eighteen years old, maybe nineteen. He talked about some of the players I'd only just heard of: Kid Ory, Bunk Johnson, Joe Oliver.

"But it was the young man himself who impressed me most," he went on, excited, "such energy and fire! Armstrong he said his name was. Louis Armstrong and a friend called me yesterday to say he's now with the Kid Ory band, full time. That's why I'm trying – not much good, I'm afraid, but Louis Armstrong told me: with time he said, it just grabs you, those were his words: it grabs you."

"Well done, Vennick, well done. I can believe that you have started on a love of something that will last you a lifetime."

"It will, sir, I know. Second only to calculus, of course."

"Of course!" Turnbull proclaimed. "Second only to calculus and to complex numbers!

"Finally, Gatsby, you must meet our singer – or vocalist, they sometimes say in America – this is Margaret Wellesley."

The young woman stepped forward, also holding out a hand, which I shook and was surprised by the firm intentionality of her handshake.

"Madge," she said, "everyone calls me Madge. It used to be Daisy but now it's Madge."

The mention of the name flicked a mental picture to my brain: Daisy Fay. This was no Daisy Fay.

"I'm glad to meet you, Madge," I said with a kind of unintended carefulness.

She was perhaps twenty-years old, tall and slim, with reddish bobbed hair, spectacles, and blue stockings. She resembled one or two of the other girls I had seen in my perambulations round the city. Her face was an almost perfect geometrical oval, her eyes disproportionately large and very candid. As I looked at her, she appeared not to blink at all, but rather to examine my own features as if they were required for a future telling. The pale blue pupils were attractively enlarged by the lenses of her spectacles.

"So you're at Trinity?" she said. "I expect you'll get to know Johnny Cusworth, he's at Trinity and, I think, a distant cousin of my family. He's fixing some jazz thing too – pretty ambitious. I think they're calling it *Jazz à Spires*. I've said I'll sing."

"And you?" I asked still impressed by the way that this self-assured and very English young woman could make sense of *Baby, won't you please come home*. "What do you do otherwise – than sing, I mean?"

"I'm at Somerville," she said. "Well, we've been in Oriel for the past months but we're gradually moving back. The war, you know. The college was used for the wounded and others with problems – Siegfried Sassoon – quite right too, but, like I said we're moving back. We don't do degrees, of course, not allowed for women."

"Next year will be different," Turnbull said with a forced kind of energy. "The ladies will be admitted at last. Degrees for all!"

I had known no young woman like the young woman in front of me: free in her appearance, by which I mean she fashionably bobbed her hair but took no pains for lipstick or powder. She spoke with all the confidence of a young man from the best of English schools. She sang jazz and sang it well – but did all these independent young women have to wear blue stockings? And spectacles? Were these, somehow, their badges of claim?

"What are you studying?" I asked her.

"Philosophy and English Literature.

"You'll know Kant of course, and the *Critique of Practical*

Reason- Kritik der prektischen Vernunft – and I'm looking into, well obviously, the categorical imperative."

I could only laugh and I was pleased to see she laughed with me.

I said, "I came through here because I heard you singing – heard you singing *Baby, won't you please come home.* That's my level, I'm afraid. I don't believe I've ever heard of... was it... Kant? Or the critic of whatever it was."

"No reason why you should. What is it you're reading?" She looked amiable and easy to befriend.

"Reading?" I was puzzled. "Some time back I read the novel for that silent movie, you know? Zane Grey? *The Lone Star Ranger*? If I recall, there was Will Farnum as the good guy and Louise Lovely as the girl he gets at the end. Maybe you saw it – in some ways inspirational. Don't be beaten – go for what you want, all that kind of thing."

She smiled: "I'm sorry. We have some odd sayings and practices here. If someone asks you what you are reading, they mean what are you studying?"

As a rule I do not blush. I do not often blush because my states of embarrassment were sublimated long since when I was sailing out with Dan Cody and piecing my slow identity together. But this time it may have been the case that I blushed.

"Nothing's fixed," I told her. "I was more or less compelled to come over here, a sort of agreement between our military, your government and the English universities – well, Oxford anyway. My name was put down before I knew it. I'm looking forward to it of course."

Mr. Turnbull came over to us. He smiled broadly.

"I'm sure you'd like to hear some more, Gatsby, what?"

I nodded and smiled to Madge Wellesley.

"You know *Beale Street Blues*?" she asked, her eyes, through the spectacles, shining into my own.

"You bet!"

"Then hold on to your seat," she grinned. "It's my best – at least I think so. Sad and what do they say – sassy..."

Still somewhat to my sense of surreal disbelief the mathematical fellow of St John's College took to the piano and went into the slow but catching rhythm of the song. Madge Wellesley sang. She may not quite have been Gilda Gray in *Schubert's Gaieties*, but she was good. She took it easy, as they say. She loved the words. She offered it straight out to whoever was listening, a gift, a poem of its kind.

She swayed gently to the chorus and in its own way it was true magic:

If Beale Street could talk, if Beale Street could talk,
Married men would have to take their beds and walk.
Except one or two, who never drink booze
And the blind man at the corner
Who sings the Beale Street Blues.

The piano, the bass, the clarinet, played smooth and sorrowing the final bars. She stepped down and came face to face.

"What did you think?"

"I loved it. You have talent. Forgive me if that sounds pompous but I have to say it. You could make a living back in..."

"I think not," she said quickly with a short laugh. "I have so much work and reading to do around Kant and the European novel. This is fun, of course. I love jazz. Now I do have to go. Why not look in at Somerville sometime – we're moving back from Oriel – and have a sherry or something. I have some records too – would you believe I have the original *Livery Stable Blues* by the Original Dixie Land Jazz Band. It was a present when I was eighteen."

"I believe I heard it. I'd love to come," I hesitated. "Could you tell me please – I mean, this is not the first time I have been invited – but... what exactly do you mean by "sherry"?"

There was no trace of condescension, only friendly information in her answer.

"So sorry – again! We ask each other round for a sherry when we would just like one or two people to come for a chat. Sherry is a blended Spanish wine and comes from the Jerez district of Spain, I believe – though I'm not quite sure."

"Any good? I mean the – sherry?"

"It can be quite boring, but experts know the subtle differences between one and another and all the colleges here have sherry as a kind of drink before food."

"Then I'd love to come for sherry."

She suggested a date, a morning at eleven thirty at Somerville College.

The band musicians, including Mr. Turnbull, shook my hand in turn. The young men wore pretty well identical clothes I noticed: flannel trousers, blazers, and similar neckties in dark blue with a shield which I took to be the college arms, red with a black rim and stars and a black lion in one corner.

"We'll be hoping to play regularly," Ewan said, "come at any time. It will help Vennick to gain confidence – nothing like an audience."

I turned to go. On the way to the lodge and the opening into St Giles I heard sharp footsteps behind me. I turned and it was a smiling Madge Wellesley.

"I did mean it, of course," she said. "I really would love to see you again."

I thanked her once more and asked the gentleman in the lodge by the gate which was the best way to Trinity College.

"Just round the corner, sir," he said. "Turn left out of here and follow the pavement round. You pass Balliol but don't let that put you off, sir, a Trinity man, just carry on and you'll come to the gates and the garden. You can't miss it."

I thanked him too, took careful hold of my luggage which contained some two thousand five hundred pounds, and prepared my mind for Trinity College.

That short walk brought back some of the trepidations I had felt earlier. Young women here were studying incomprehensible German philosophy while singing jazz and the blues. The men all appeared to be so rich that they never gave a thought of wealth. Teachers – or fellows as they were confusingly called – did mathematics, calculus and chamber music with jazz, and something called *lieder*.

True, I had my own story ready by now – fiction maybe but soon to be realized as fact. I already had the first installment of what promised to be the necessary fortune to secure Daisy Fay. Despite everything, Daisy Fay was all I wished to acquire.

I turned into Broad Street, and as had been warned, the first college I passed was Balliol though I could not understand why this should "put me off". Passing Balliol College, I could not fail to notice a curious setting of bricks and stones in the roadway, a cross in a circle, emblematic no doubt of something but it meant nothing I could understand. A few steps further and I was in front of the gates of Trinity College, tall iron bars reaching high, topped with some insignia of the college: elegant, I thought, yet strong – a good precedent, I might hope, for the weeks ahead.

I paused in front of the tall gates and looked in.

Directly before me was a pathway alongside a lawn with trees. The grass and the trees were well tended, better I noted than in Hyde Park or Kensington Gardens during my brief climb into those enclosures. Then I had assumed, as was so general, that the toll of the war had made the usual care and attention difficult. Who was to blame for a little neglect after so much upheaval?

Here, however, at first sight certainly, the front quadrangle of Trinity College was well cared for.

Ahead of me, at the top of the pathway that stretched from the gate, was what I took to be a chapel. There were large and no doubt stained glass windows and a square tower with its own separate window, beneath which a clock told me the time of the afternoon. Beneath this tower was an archway, dark and somewhat obscure, which I supposed led into the main buildings of the college.

I could not help noticing that the stonework of the building ahead, if it was the chapel, was in some need of repair, as were the outer walls of the smaller buildings along Broad Street on the other side of the college entrance.

I stood for several minutes staring into what I took to be my home for the coming weeks. One or two students in blazers and flannel trousers sauntered around the front quadrangle. They carried wooden bats which I guessed at once were for playing cricket, broader in the body than our baseball bats, flat fronted though curved or thickened at the back. I decided instantly that I, the new Gatsby, would learn to play cricket and become a reasonable player. The vision of a cloistered monkish institution of incantations and solitary silence vanished at once, blown off with the beauty of this view, the beauty of these young men and their sport, the beauty of a fresh anticipation.

As I turned away from the large gate my eye looked further down Broad Street. I saw an inn sign which had the words and picture of a white horse. I also saw, to the right on the far side, a tall stone building, with a curious dome-like structure like a crown in white and green, but most noticeably surrounded by a metal fencing topped by the heavy sculptured busts of the twelve apostles.

It was almost as if I was postponing a baptismal moment. I walked on, beyond Trinity, and entered *The White Horse* inn. It was below sidewalk level, down steps and through an ancient door on the right. Inside there was a flow of daylight, just, from the sidewalk of Broad Street, but there were also electric lamps, candles and one or two strategic oil-lamps. There were seats along the walls, not unlike the pews in American churches, small tables, even a small fire at the far end, wood logs in a tiny steel grate below a small chimney, cheerful and cracking.

A young man was sitting there alone, half turned away from me, gazing still and silent into the small flames.

"Yes, sir, what would you like?" The woman at the bar was no longer young but strikingly beautiful, Italian-looking with a shine of dark hair and wide brown eyes, somewhat exotic in gold earrings and with an embroidered puff-sleeved blouse in green and gold.

"I'd like a beer, please."

"Certainly. What sort of beer would you like?"

I remembered *The Eagle and the Child* and asked if she had Brakspear. She laughed.

"I can tell where you're from," she said, "by your voice. But you've been here before."

She had picked up a metal tankard and was levering the beer into it.

"I have to admit," I said with a smile. "I was in *The Eagle and the Child* earlier. I had my first Brakspear then."

"Excuse me," she said with a frown which still grinned, "it's *The Eagle and Child*, sir, if you don't mind – not *The Eagle and THE Child*. And the young fellows call it *The Bird and Baby* – so's you'll know."

"Thank you so much," I said with exaggerated courtesy. "I shall make a point of never forgetting that as long as I live."

"That'll be fourpence ha'penny, thank you, sir. It's quality stuff is Brakspear."

I took hold of the pint, looked towards the window.

"Can you tell me why there's the busts of the twelve apostles across the road there, ma'am?"

She followed my gaze.

"Oh, they're not the twelve apostles, young man, they're the Roman emperors, but lord only knows which is which 'cos I don't and that's for sure. Someone came in here and told me a story the other day, said that someone had seen those same emperors crying their eyes out. I think it was baloney mind you."

From her speech I realized that, despite appearances, she was not Italian.

"May I ask where you are from? If that isn't discourteous..."

"No, quite a lot of the lads ask that. Nothing special, mind. I'm from Abingdon, I don't know if you know it."

"I'm afraid not."

She gave me another smile and wiped the bar. I took the

beer to the window and stayed perhaps for half an hour and more sipping from the glass, watching the people in the street pass by – an interesting array of boots, patent leather shoes, high heels and even Roman sandals.

Finishing the drink I gave the glass back to the woman behind the counter.

"See you again?"

"Most likely. I'm at Trinity next door."

"'Bye for now then."

I lit a cigarette outside the White Horse, standing alone on the sidewalk. Two or three inhalations and that was enough. I retraced my steps towards the entrance of Trinity College.

Turning once more I saw a street ahead of me, opposite the big gates of Trinity. I crossed as if once more postponing my Trinity baptism.

The street was called Turl Street, narrow and congested with motors, bicycles and a couple of horse drawn carts. I walked its length and found that it came to a larger main road, the High Street, and facing me on the far sidewalk was a double bow-windowed tailors' shop, *Hall Brothers* said the sign, and there was an insignia of some kind – three plumes and the words *Ich Dien* – but, most notably, there was a spectacular hat in the window.

It had the shape of a top hat though with a shallower crown. The rims at each side curved more boldly upward than top hats do, but, best of all, it looked from where I stood as if it had been made from pure gold.

Curiosity forced me to enter the small shop, a doorbell rang, and a short man with pince-nez approached me, a tape measure at the ready round his neck.

"Yes, sir?"

"It's just the hat in the window," I said, "it caught my eye. Could you give me an idea of its cost?"

"With pleasure, sir. Allow me."

He opened glass doors which enclosed the window space, reached in and handed me the gold hat.

"Do try it, sir. You are very welcome."

There was a looking glass against one wall. I stepped towards it, hat in hand, smoothed my hair with my right hand and placed the hat carefully on my head.

"Perfect, sir, if I might say so. It could have been made for you, sir."

I looked with as much detachment as I could at my reflection in the glass. It was true that the gold hat fitted me comfortably. The low crown and the upward curve of the rims, left and right, seemed somehow to harmonize well with my rather square features.

"Don't you agree, sir, it could have been designed precisely for your good self?"

I carefully removed the hat and handed it to the tailor.

"Is it actual gold?"

"There is gold thread, sir, and silk that has been specially woven, having been previously dyed with an oriental compound which makes silk permanently sheened like gold itself. The frame-work of the hat, which keeps it in shape, you could describe as a gold alloy, sir. It is, I understand from its maker, entirely unique."

"It must be very expensive, I guess."

"It is expensive, sir. But how often do we come across a gold hat, what?"

I hesitated. "What is the price?"

"It's ninety guineas, sir."

"Guineas?" I was still unsure.

"Ninety-four pounds, ten shillings, sir."

"That's around a hundred and sixty dollars?"

"If you say so, sir."

I smoothed the silk sides of the hat with my palm. It felt right somehow as a symbol – not a crown exactly, or a coronet, but a gold hat to be worn with a determination to shine, and to win. I replaced it briefly on my head and took another look in the glass. It did seem so completely right for me to wear it and I wondered what Daisy Fay would say when or if she ever saw me in it.

"Ninety-four pounds and ten shillings?"

"Yes, sir. If you are a member of one of the colleges, sir, you could, of course, open an account with us."

"I shall have to think it over. I like it, I have to say. But I should like to think it over."

"As you think best, sir." He replaced the hat on its stand in the window, and closed the glass partition. "Don't take too long thinking about it, sir. Knowing the young men today and the clamor for glamour and originality I expect someone will be buying it quite soon."

"I shall not delay," I said, "and thank you for your help."

I crossed the High Street and walked briskly down Turl Street again, back towards Trinity. A new and wondering energy seemed to have possessed me, and I could only think that it was wearing the gold hat that might have done it, affected my mood, given me grace.

"Yes, sir?"

Once again a genial face looked at me through the window of the lodge – this time, and finally, my destination: Trinity College, Isaac Newton, apples, and a new life.

"My name is Gatsby," I said. "Jay Gatsby. I believe I am expected."

Chapter 4

Will these people, these experiences – I asked myself the question as I stood at the entrance to Trinity College – will they add anything to me, to the making of Gatsby – or will they take things from me?

"Gatsby," I repeated. Then I spelled it out: "G, A, T, S, B, Y."

He looked at a list.

"Mr. Gatsby. Major Gatsby. Quite right, sir. And may I say welcome? I believe you are in Set 64 in staircase 12, sir. Your scout is Cadman, sir. Richard Cadman. He was fighting too, you understand. Young and prepared. And here he is."

A sturdy, thickset, open faced young man, even younger than myself, had approached the lodge. I recognized him as the man who had been by the fire in *The White Horse* just a short time before.

"I'm your scout, sir. Cadman. Some call me Cadders and I do not mind. Your room's ready, sir, and I've left a kettle of hot water if you want a wash and shave. The baths are at the back."

I held out a hand.

"It's good to meet you, Mr. Cadman."

His expression was set and solid, somehow inspirational of loyalty and trust.

"Cadman, sir," he said firmly. "Just Cadman. Or Cadders behind my back if you so wish."

He had already picked up my luggage – including the quantity of cash – and was off at some speed towards my staircase.

"What do you mean by a set?" I asked the porter.

"Well, it's rooms if you like, sir. Sometimes, and probably very soon, people will have to share. But for now you're in a set of your own, sir. Staircase 12."

"Thank you again."

"The President will want to see you, sir. I think there's a note in your pigeon hole."

"My what?"

"Your pigeon hole, sir. If you wish you can come through that door into the lodge here and you'll find what we call pigeon holes – open boxes, you might say, where we put messages and letters and things."

I stepped through the door which, with its two-halved horizontal opening, reminded me of a stable door, like those we had in North Dakota for horses to lean through. Inside there was indeed a positive honeycomb of pigeon holes, each with a name in alphabetic order, GATSBY quite prominent. Somewhat to my surprise and pleasure there were messages for me in my pigeon hole. I took them and asked the porter the way to my set, or rooms.

Cadman was in the rooms before me. He had placed my luggage on the small and narrow bed, and opened one of the windows which looked out on to a very extensive and beautiful garden with long lawns which stretched down to another large metal gate.

"There have not been many gentlemen in college in recent months, sir," Cadman told me, "though the number is improving now by the week. During the war – I was away fighting myself – we got down to just a handful of gentlemen, so many of the rooms were used by the military, sir. Some still are. There's a kettle of hot water like I said. Anything you want you can find me in my cubby-hole at the bottom of staircase ten. For the baths you go through the passage at the corner of the quad."

He turned, almost militarily, and left. Then came back a moment later.

"You will like this place, sir, if I may say so. It is loyal, civilized, and inspiring. They gave my wife an allowance of seven shillings each week while I was away fighting. It is the sort of place you can never forget – or disown."

I thought he was standing to attention as he spoke, and the speech did not come easily to him. I also thought that before turning away this young twenty-year-old was about to salute, but he simply turned and left me and watching him go I can only say that I felt a kind of almost family affection.

I went up close to the window. The view was truly inspiring to me at that moment, as the nights would be later and in the worst of pain.

Gatsby at Trinity!

As I have said, I choose not to recall my past too much. Yet I could not, if only for a moment, but wonder how my father, poor on his farmland in the United States of America, would think of this, my new home. It was welcome – the time, I mean, and the place. I would never choose to make too much of it, but from this moment on Gatsby was, in truth, an Oxford man.

I unpacked the clothes I had brought, satisfied now only with the jacket bought for me months before by Dan Cody and the elegant pants I had purchased in The Strand in London. Other things would be useful but I would need more. I would acquire blazers and flannels, a decent suit and possibly a dinner jacket or even tails. I had half decided that the gold hat in the window of *Hall Brothers* in the High Street would be mine.

Feelings of certainty and an encompassed joy flowed through me as I gazed at the Trinity garden. On some nights, I decided, I would rise from bed in the dark hours, leave my room and walk into the Trinity garden. There I would stretch out on the beautifully cropped grass and I would look to the sky and the moon and the stars, and make this corner of a foreign field forever mine and my American dream.

There was a letter from Daisy Fay among those I had taken from my pigeon hole at the lodge. It was brief:

"Dearest, dearest Jay Gatsby, I can never put you out of my mind and the love we share seems to me to be growing ever stronger. I have discovered that you are in Oxford, England, and the thought of this delights me.

"Think of me please, for I miss you and trust that our separation will not now be for too long.

"Young men invite me to many dances and parties, of course, and I do not mind accompanying them – but it is always the thought of my love for you which goes with me constantly.

"As I write this to you I can smell the sweet scent of orchids by my side – I am in the lobby of the Chesterton Hotel – and hear an orchestra playing in the restaurant. It is tea time. I am alone, although my mother will be joining me soon. People pass my table, their faces like rose petals blown by a soft wind, so elegant, so fair.

"Be with me soon, Jay Gatsby.

"You are missed so much.

"From your own love, Daisy."

Another thicker envelope, sealed in the old-fashioned way with red wax and the imprint of a personal cipher, had a typed note which was signed by Borson Slagle.

"It is important that you bank most of the money you have with you at the office of Fox Chicago Lester which you will be able to locate above the Windermere Studios in George Street. This will be deposited in your name at another address back home in Chicago, with drawing rights in New York and Detroit.

"I am told that the prohibition laws will be in full effect from January next year and it is expected that when you return from England you will be able to occupy yourself full-time with setting up an alternative supply system for liquor in all parts of the Union.

"Meanwhile note that the investments from the former German bonds are doing well. Among those we have taken up and reinvested the following results have been declared:

"*Baldwin Locomotive* rose from 72 to 93, *General Motors* from 130 to 191, *United States Steel* from 90 to 1041/2, and *International Mercantile Marine* from 23 to 475/8.

"I have also been told to inform you that your name and status as a war hero are even more helpful than was expected towards the good financial results for our undertakings so far. You are trusted.

"Destroy this note when you have fully assimilated its contents,

"Borson Slagle."

Among the other messages for me was one of formality which said that the President of Trinity College, President Blakiston, would be pleased to welcome me personally to Trinity College if I would contact his secretary and clerk, Mr. Mounsey, to arrange an appropriate time.

Though my name had been written by hand on this invitation, and with a carefully calligraphic pen, the card itself was immaculately embossed with the coat-of arms of the college – which I still took to be the heads of dragons – and enriched with engraved printing.

It felt appropriate to stand this card conspicuously on the shelf above the fireplace in my new rooms, or my "set" – where young Cadman had already lit a tiny smoking blaze of welcome – and I placed the President's invitation accordingly in this conspicuous place.

As I did so, there was a knock on the door and a very tall young man entered without waiting for my answer.

"You're Gatsby, yes? Jolly good, jolly good.

"The name's Cusworth, Johnny Cusworth, heard you were here, jolly good, jolly good.

"Others'll be saying it but I wanted to be the first, what? Jolly good show, Gatsby. Great to have you here. Hope you can stay for a good while. Too young to fight myself, but the word got around about you and the Argonne Forest. Lost a lot of our own chaps too, y'know. Let me shake your hand, Gatsby."

The effusion was overwhelming, or at least it took me aback for a moment. I conjectured this young man was not yet twenty years old, yet he exuded an energy and confidence which was infectious – and likeable.

He was tall, extremely tall, so that I had to set my chin upwards to look at him as we shook hands. His eyes were wide and blue, not unlike those of a child at its happiest investigative times. His cheeks shone and were aglow with pink as if from a fell-walk through the wind.

"Johnny Cusworth, old sport, like I said. I got in here because I'm not bad at rugger, I've rowed a bit too, cricket comes easily, I can organize music and stuff, and, if you don't ask too much, I can just about parse a verse or two of Ovid."

"Are you studying... are you *reading*... Latin then?"

He laughed.

"You could say that, old sport. At Eton they do a good job turning out chaps who can cope a bit with just about anything. Saw that in the war, of course. Me father was here, you see, and it's kind of the family tradition. His grandfather was a Trinity man too, y'know, and so it goes on.

"That's why chaps like you are such a great thing to have with us? Spice in the soup, you might say, what? Where're you from, may I ask?"

"San Francisco."

"Heard of it. Never been. Done much shootin'?"

"Well, in France, of course... the Germans..."

"Sorry, old sport didn't mean the war, of course. Just wondered whether you might come up to the Lodge sometime and come out with the shotguns, horses too."

I was guessing now. I had ridden horses in the army but this lodge, this college...?

"The lodge – isn't that the porters'..."

He laughed and was so young and free as he did so.

"Good one, that Gatsby, jolly good one! I can just see 'em! All the scouts–Cadders in the lead, eh?–the head porter and the head cook, all galloping across the Yorkshire moors..."

"It sounds fun."

"Fun? It'd be hilarious, old sport. Like jazz, do you?"

"Very much. I think I caught your name earlier. St John's?"

"Oh goodness me, yes! Gosh, I've missed it! Meant to go! Weren't Madge Wellesley and Dickie Delmore doing something there earlier on?"

"I happened to be passing. They mentioned you..."

"Quite right too! I'm fixing a jazz thing called *Jazz à Spires* – 'aspires' you see. Jazz, see, and Oxford spires? We're fixing a miniature model of all the college chapels, domes, spires and everything, as a kind of background for the music. You'll see it in the quad if you haven't noticed it already. Most of the music'll be American, of course, but... well, do you play, Gatsby?"

"I'm afraid not."

"Don't worry, old sport. We'll show you. Have you on the drums in no time, what? Have you time for a drink or something? You'll be in Hall later, I expect. There's still only about sixty of us, so the more the merrier. What do you say?"

"I must just go out for a while, I'm afraid... on a bit of business," I said. "And the President asked me to fix an appointment with him too."

"Good man, the Prezz. Really cares, y'know. Well, make yourself at home, old sport, do whatever you have to do and maybe we could see you in Hall for dinner, what?"

He smiled as he turned to leave, and once again *Oh, you English!* came into my head. In some way hard to define I felt deeply and proudly American in the presence of people like this man, Johnny Cusworth. I say hard to define, but perhaps not impossible. Americans in my own experience, from the poverty circles of my earliest years in North Dakota to the travels I made with Dan Cody, and the very short times in New York or elsewhere, are on the whole easy and relaxed. We are, as I have said, a young people with the future still ahead of us to shape and to make our own. I had heard the word *teenager* used occasionally, but only in America, never in England. It was a kind of sub-culture for the separated young. An English teenager was totally impossible and always would be – especially among these sophisticated Trinity men. Certainly many Americans do not, as yet, have the rituals of the Europeans, a seniority of ritual which I found in France and even, in their own ways, in the Liverpool pubs and the London I briefly saw before I came to Oxford. It was a ritual, I conjectured, of two thousand years of practice and habit. We Americans are not so predetermined. Yet for some of the English, and this man Cusworth showed it conspicuously, there was a kind of relaxation of identity that eased through the formalities of speech and left the hearer warm and charmed. It was my American character that loved it, though I could never show this here.

"Hey, bud, how're you doin'?" one American might call to another, and the cheer and amiability are fine.

Yet, "good afternoon, sir, I hope you are well and it gives me great pleasure to have you here with us," formal in tone and construct, somehow hit me as being every bit as chummy in its wordy concern.

I already knew then that I liked these English.

As already noted, I had an involuntary tendency to soften my American speech and to mouth some of the English talk I was hearing. Their language brought a new and unforced beauty to my ears, if also a self-consciousness to my own speech. True, in Liverpool I had thought at first they were speaking Irish or some foreign tongue, and the porter at Euston station was incomprehensible. The songs in *The Mikado*, however – though not altogether to my taste for what I guessed would become a jazz age – nevertheless stroked my hearing with its delicious touch: the diction, the registers, the tone were so englishly right.

I had never heard anyone talk quite like Johnny Cusworth – not even in the few plays I had ever seen on stage, and they were few indeed, where actors played English gentlemen or ladies with ambitious accents. With Cusworth, I enjoyed the "old sport" stuff and the "jolly goods", perhaps even tempted to try them myself.

When Cusworth left my rooms I took the packet of money from my bag and counted off, from the bundle of five-pound Bank of England notes, two thousand pounds. This still left me with a few hundred and I concealed these under the carpet in a corner of my room, placing a chair over the spot for safety.

Then, leaving Trinity, I asked the gentleman at the lodge which was the way to George Street and he waved a free arm:

"Turn right here, sir, and then straight on. You can't miss it, just the other side of the Cornmarket."

The Windermere Studios were not hard to find. It was harder to determine what kind of studios they were. Nude models in red clay could be seen through the half curtained windows, as could hand-made plates and what I guessed were tea-pots. There were also some leather-bound books on shelves, embroidered shawls, table lamps with decorated parchment shades, and what I took to be a solid marble bust of William Shakespeare.

Alongside the door of the Studios ran a small passage with a stairway and a tiny card with an upward-pointing arrow that read *Fox Chicago Lester, please ring*. There was a pull-cord for a bell, which I pulled hard, hearing a distant ring. A moment later a dark-suited man, perhaps a little younger than me, appeared at the top of the stairs.

"Major Gatsby?" he asked. I nodded.

"Please come up, major." I followed him to what must have been the attic of the building and into a small, stuffy and rather dirty dark office with a desk, a telephone and two chairs.

"Please take a seat," he said, opening a drawer and taking out a bottle and two glasses which he set on the desk in front of him. "Would you like a Scotch?"

"I won't, thank you," I said.

He gestured to himself and the glass: "You don't mind...?"

"No, please. Go ahead."

He poured out a half glass of whiskey and carefully replaced the bottle in his desk.

"You have the money, major?"

"I brought some of the money," I said, "I also kept a little for my own expenses."

"Quite right, quite right. For the money you give to me I shall give you a receipt and it will be yours, in your name, but in an account in America. My instructions are to reassure you that your name and signature are proving invaluable to the business projects that are underway.

"An account has already been opened in your name – Jay Gatsby – and funds will continue to be added, as a form of commission, until you are able to return to America yourself and then to take on, full-time, the business of expansion – along the lines which, I believe, have been intimated to you.

"I might explain that my name is Cecil Parke. I have connections with Merton College, but I too shall be per-manently based in America in a few weeks time and expect to play a part in the expansion of our concerns.

"Are there any questions, major?"

I said, "I seem to have done very little – I mean, to earn the commission, as you call it, that I have already been paid."

"That is most certainly not the case, sir. It has been thanks to the fact that we have been able to cite you as a participant in our activities that many, who might otherwise have been reluctant, are co-operating in every way with the expansion and the contacts we require."

"Can you give me any idea of what happens when I leave here, when I get back to America?"

"As far as I understand it, major, it will be very much left to yourself. You will, one might say, be 'your own man' and free to work in whichever cities you prefer. The opportunities, we know, are – well – explosive. With the aftermath of war, the tide of fresh and remunerative bonds, the prohibition proposals, the huge and likely expansions... some of our colleagues are already well into the millionaire class."

Daisy! Daisy! Daisy Fay! Her name, her face, her long kissing came to my mind at that moment.

In that dingy office in Oxford I perceived the great future we would one day share, the gardens and the lawns, bigger, broader, greener even than the Trinity lawns, the opulence, the clothes, the automobiles, the travel, and the music, the jazz, the frivolity and the joy. Daisy! The very name was like an invocation or a prayer: eternal certainty!

"There are just a few more papers for you to sign, Major Gatsby," Cecil Parke was saying, "and then everything is up to date.

"When you sign these you can expect that by the end of May – let us say around Friday the thirtieth – something close to a million dollars will be waiting in your account in America. That is the estimated return on the liquor purchases since the Eighteenth Amendment has been confirmed as part of the constitution by a thirty-sixth state."

Legality or illegality did not enter my mind, and I did not care. Only a few months before I had heard the daily screams and the poundings, the sludge and blood, and seen the imprisoned future, dark, gated and unobtainable, in the last days of battle. I had personally been in command and therefore responsible for the killing of hundreds of young Germans by my own machine-gun battalion. The screams and shouts of horror in the German language were, for some reason, even more unforgettable than our own, the terror of a foreign boy calling for his mother or his god rings forever. Now, therefore, I had to be the shaper of things, no longer the mere obedient: of myself, my future, my life and my status as Apollo for Daisy.

I signed all the papers that Parke presented to me.

"I have the feeling, Major Gatsby, that you are going to do really well. Mr. Wolfshiem praises you to the skies, you might say. He thinks you should join the American Legion when you get back, and also do something for a friend of his in Albany – but all that's for later. Good luck now!"

We shook hands.

"Oh and drop into the library at Merton if you ever feel inclined. I'm often there. It would be good to see you again, to keep in touch."

I made a half-promise and descended the dark staircase down to George Street. On the corner of the Cornmarket there was now a barrel organ and a young woman singing:

In quaint native dress an Italian maid
Was deep in distress as the streets she strayed
Searching in every part
For her false sweetheart
And his ice-cream cart.
Her English was bad it cannot be denied
And so to herself in Italian she cried...

My feelings of optimism and certainty made me take a gold sovereign from my pocket and put it in the bowl on the organ. The young woman grinned and winked. I winked back. She looked straight at me and sang:

Oh, Oh, Antonio he's gone away,
Left me alonio, all on my ownio,
I want to meet him with his new sweetheart,
Then up will go Antonio and his ice-cream cart.

Back in Trinity I found Mr. Mounsey in his office in the front quadrangle or quad as I was teaching myself to say. He was a bright, squirrel-like, darting man of near middle age, with a smile so strong that it forced his eyes to close in sympathy. In front of him was one of the latest bow-fronted Imperial Typewriters.

"It's a Model B," he said with a smile of pride when he saw me notice it – that and a bunch of violets in a small vase.

"The President is looking forward so much to meeting you properly, Mr. Gatsby," he told me warmly, "perhaps this afternoon. Tea perhaps? He's a busy man, as you know, Vice-Chancellor too, of course, but I know that he puts meeting you a priority for his diary."

We settled for a later time for me to see President Blakiston and he wrote it neatly in the diary on his desk.

In the front quad I met Norrington again.

"All booked in?" he said with a smile. "May I make a suggestion? We've just started a new thing, a new group, club if you like. It's restricted in number but I know you'd be welcome.

"We call it the *Thirteen Club*. One of the chaps reads a paper he has written. The others listen. Then we discuss it, and there's a good smack of port doing the rounds while this goes on.

"Chap called Sassoon might be coming this time. He's been in the war, wounded, emotional problems, was in

Somerville for hospitalization, writes poetry and offers to read a paper on poetry and war. You'd be welcome, Gatsby."

I said that I would be pleased to be there and the amiable and friendly Norrington scribbled and signed an invitation card which he gave to me.

There was little time between now and my meeting with the President. I decided once more to stroll Oxford for a while, finding myself eventually at Somerville College where I would also soon be visiting Madge Wellesley. There were distinct signs of its use as a hospital.

Nurses in uniform and doctors in white coats came and went through the entrance at the bottom of what I found was Woodstock Road. One or two young men in white shirts, red ties and with crutches were making their way around the front quad.

"Don't I know you?"

Someone touched my arm, gently gripping the sleeve, and making to turn me round. It was a woman's voice.

A young nurse, pretty and tanned, looked at me with astonishment. She was familiar.

"It is you! It is you, yes?"

Her large dark eyes were alight with humor.

"I'm sorry, I can't..."

"We danced!" she said, so excitedly that people on the other side of the Woodstock Road turned to see that she was in no trouble. She had a strong but attractive accent.

"We danced together! Well..." she smiled, "you *tried* to dance. Remember? You must remember?"

She started to sway and step in rhythm in her nurse's uniform around the gate of Somerville.

She paused. "Now I am a nurse here, see! I volunteer for training. Just here." She pointed. "The Radcliffe

Infirmary. I came from Praia. Santiago. Cape Verde. You must remember. Here!"

She took my hand and pulled me towards her, starting to sway and swing to the music in her head, there on the sidewalk. A small group of nurses, doctors, students and the walking wounded now clustered at the entrance of Somerville to watch us.

"The *coladeira*!" she said at the top of her voice. "You are Jimmy and I am, Mayra, remember? We dance the *coladeira* together in Praia!"

Of course! That the world could shrink through wars and the aftermath of wars was evidenced here.

"Come for a coffee. We have canteen."

She took my arm and led me through the Radcliffe Infirmary, alongside Somerville College, and insisted on buying me what was perhaps the worst cup of coffee I have ever had in my life. She herself was radiant still with sun and beauty.

We talked eagerly and fast, and I told her about the rest of my travels with Dan Cody, about the war, and about the compelled studying I was now doing in Oxford. She told me how cousins had travelled to Europe, how they had told her about all the young men dying and wounded, and how she had decided to volunteer, first for routine work with the Red Cross, and then to train as "a proper nurse".

"We must meet again soon," she said, getting up and explaining that she had a patient to visit in Somerville next door.

"We must do that," I said.

I sat for a moment alone in the canteen. If some other girl, some authentically radiant young girl who gave me a fresh glance... one moment, a magical encounter... could blot out... No! Daisy! Daisy alone and true!

It was late afternoon, almost evening, when I at last walked up the main steps of the President's lodgings in the front quad of Trinity. I pressed a bell and it was President Blakiston himself who answered the door.

"Do come in, Gatsby, do come in. It is so good to have you here. You had a decent journey I take it?"

I followed him into the hallway, noting the upwards staircase lined with framed portraits, and then through to what I guessed was his study.

Since I had arrived I had found many of the buildings in Trinity somewhat dilapidated or in disrepair which I considered to be understandable in view of the war and the effects this must have had on the college finances and upkeep. The chapel walls were pitted and broken and to the right of the front quadrangle building works of some kind were in progress.

The President's study on the other hand was neat and attractive with its furnishings and pictures.

There were one or two original paintings, but no photographs of a wife or of children.

Dr Blakiston took his seat behind the carved and dignified desk, the seat being a wooden and leathered chair with a high back.

For a moment, perhaps as long as for half a minute he simply looked at me, there where I was standing, somewhat awkwardly, in the middle of the room.

"You make it something like seventy-nine, I think, Gatsby."

"I'm sorry, sir?"

"If my maths and update are correct you are probably the seventy-ninth man we have in the college now, not counting the SCR."

"The SCR, sir?"

"The Senior Common Room, Gatsby. The fellows."

"Of course, sir, the fellows." I remembered that much.

"Perhaps you'll be good enough to tell me a little about yourself. I might mention that when it was decided by the American military that you would be chosen to come here, we also had a personal note from the White House, from President Wilson himself, and a more informal note from..." he looked down at his desk, "a Captain Harry Truman who fought with you, I believe, in a crucial battle."

"That's correct, sir. Truman and his men did great things. Some have said that it was the final battle to end the war. We were fighting, along with Australians, French and English of course, from the twenty-sixth of September last year to the eleventh of November."

"It was called? Remind me?"

"They called it the Argonne Forest battle, sir, that's the territory we had to win. We did win it. We lost – it was tragic – we lost thousands of men. But we were told that it was the largest battle in American history – a total of over a million American soldiers."

"Good heavens! The numbers, Gatsby, the numbers! And your family, what did they make of all this, of what you did?"

My story was prepared – for Trinity, Oxford, and for all that would come later when wealth erased forever the poor drab boy from North Dakota.

"My family were wealthy people in the Middle West, sir," I lied. "For reasons which I would rather not recall they are now all dead – fortunately I understand there is quite a substantial sum waiting for me when I return home. Otherwise, sir, all I can say is that I have travelled extensively – Paris, Rome, Venice, painting a little here and there, sometimes game-hunting..."

"You know Paris then?" he said eagerly.

I did not wish to show ignorance, just in case, and told him that I had only passed through Paris briefly and was not very well acquainted with the city.

"So you are an orphan, Gatsby?"

"Very much so, sir, I'm afraid."

"No brothers or sisters?"

"None, sir. No relatives at all."

"I have lost three brothers of my own, you know. Tragic. And so what will you be doing when you leave Trinity, may I ask?"

"I have business plans, sir. Like I said, there is quite an investment waiting for me when I get home – and I intend to do all I can to make that prosper even further."

"Well, I wish you good fortune, Gatsby. For a young American like yourself the sky, as they say, is the limit. Who knows? President Gatsby, eh? One thing about being English, I suppose, is that there is little point in hoping to be king one day."

He laughed. I would call it a discreet laugh.

President Blakiston – who, I discovered, was a doctor of divinity – was a serious but very frail gentleman and was also, at a guess, approaching sixty years of age. He was completely bald over the forehead with an expanse of crown which to me suggested a sort of scholarship and dignity. He kept a very bushy and carefully tended moustache, and I noted that he chose to dress in the style of before the war, with turned down collar and bow tie, jacket and waistcoat of well-cut tweed, a gown of course, and noticeable cuff buttons in gold. He had a very direct and almost, but not quite, intimidating stare through the perfectly circular and wire-rimmed spectacles which he wore. Not for the first time I could not fail to contrast these Oxford-English presentations and people with the ones I had known in America.

President Blakiston and Desmond Cliffe Harrow, the head of St Olaf's Lutheran College in southern Minnesota and which I had attended for only a very short time, could not be more different. Blakiston was frail, even sickly, but robust in manner and with the scholarly confidence of learning.

Desmond Cliffe Harrow had been solid, robust, with a thick growth of red hair and an enormous red beard, muscular shoulders and a weathered skin. He also spoke loudly and evangelically whereas the doctor of divinity, here at his desk before me in Oxford, spoke with a mildness as if to a cousin or nephew.

"Have you met any of your fellow undergraduates yet?"

"One or two, sir, more or less at random, you might say. But they do seem to be very hospitable if I might say so."

"Whom have you met then?"

"Well, Norrington for one, and Cusworth dropped into my rooms, my set, to say hello."

"Excellent! Good men the two of 'em. I'm hoping that as the numbers get back to the level they were in 1914 we might at least avoid some of the troubles we had at that time."

"Troubles?"

"It was often a bit rowdy and irresponsible, Gatsby. Young men who thought they could do just whatever they liked. Fires lit in the college grounds, or even in the Broad. Fireworks, fights even. Everyone – well not quite everyone – many drunk and out of control. Noise all the time. Sometimes it looked as though the fun we often have between Balliol and ourselves could actually develop into a war of its own."

"You have been here sometime then, sir?"

"Trinity is my life, Gatsby. Some have said, behind my back of course, that I am a mean, closed-up, and book-keeping sort of person who only thinks about money and accounts. The truth is that I have had to keep this college going through all sorts of ups and downs."

"When did you first get here, sir?"

"I was fortunate to win a scholarship in 1881, classics.

"They gave me a first in 1885, then, later on, to divinity and a fellowship. This place has, literally, been my life. I became a tutor, you see. Then senior tutor, then domestic bursar, and I wrote the first ever history of the college in 1898. I've been President now for twelve years. I've been Vice-Chancellor of the university for two years already.

"The hardest times were when we got down to only nine undergraduates just over a year ago. Terrible."

"I can imagine, sir."

"So I mean to do everything in my power to restore this place to the way it deserves to be – everything, Gatsby."

He appeared to warm to his subject. He waved me to take a seat but I was conscious that I could have been anyone, or no-one, as he poured out beliefs that, for some reason, he might seldom have had the chance to express. Perhaps he thought that a young and naïve American was safe ground for such divulgences.

I noted in writing the gist of his words later. They had a passion which, I was frequently told, was just not a part of his usual character.

"This is a place of honor and history," he continued. "That is why I care for it so much. Do you know, Gatsby that eight hundred and twenty men of Trinity served in the war? Eight hundred and twenty! Of our men! And, of these, one hundred and fifty-three did not survive.

"Just think – just think as you walk through the college, this small yet beautiful assembly of buildings, that more than a hundred and fifty, just from here alone, gave their lives for their country.

"The least that I can do – and I know people scoff at my style behind my back – is to make the place fit for the sacrifice of these brave fellows."

He stopped. He stared at me for a full half minute.

Uncertain, I said nothing, looked back respectfully into his face. Then he turned his head abruptly and looked sharply through the window. He snapped back to look at me, his voice softer.

"Some say that women should be admitted to the university.

"Women have their place, I say. Their place is not on the battlefields of France – nor in the common rooms of our ancient, and masculine, universities. If women are ever fully admitted to Oxford University – and many are bidding for such a move for next year – then I believe we can say goodbye to a thousand years of English learning.

"Women have their place, I say, but if they erode the pride of the centuries this place will become a mere fashion-house, a snob's token, or a marriage market. By the way, I have something for you."

He rose from the desk, somewhat unsteadily, and crossed to a wall of drawers and shelves facing the window to the front quad.

"Knowing you were coming, and moved by the note from the American President, I thought it only right to give you a permanent keepsake of your time with us. Here it is. I have written in it. It's something I did about twenty-five years ago. Please take it – let's say it's also a small thank-you for what you did for us all last year.

"There's an expression I've heard among the undergraduates: you saved our bacon, Gatsby."

It was a book, of course.

The title was daunting – *The speeches of M. Tullius Cicero against Catiline and Antony and for Murena and Milo*. The date was 1894, the name of the translator – and thank goodness they were not in the original Latin! – was printed in gold leaf on the spine and also on the front: Herbert Edward Douglas Blakiston, the publishers, Methuen and Co, Essex Street, The Strand!

"I know you'll enjoy it, Gatsby. Several have told me from time to time that they did not know what they would have done without it. You'll find it's a good read – oh, not thanks to me, Gatsby, thanks to Cicero, of course, Cicero!"

More out of politeness than curiosity, more as formal reaction than learning, I opened the book at an early page and read:

"*How much further, Catilina, will you carry your abuse of our forbearance?*

"*How much longer will your reckless temper baffle our restraint?*

"*What bounds will you set to this display of your uncontrolled audacity?*

"*Do you not perceive that your designs are exposed?*"

"I can see I shall really enjoy reading this, sir," I said with a hoped-for scholarly relish. "Thank you very much. In time I intend to have my own library of valued books, this will certainly be among them."

"I should hope so, Gatsby, I should hope so. Now – have you decided yet what fields of study you should like to pursue?"

"Not exactly."

"Then I strongly recommend some philosophy, some classics, and possibly some literature. Your length of stay is, I believe, finally, of you own choice. Even a smattering of these subjects could last a lifetime, Gatsby. And I see you as a man who likes to make decisions for a life-time."

Mr. Mounsey brought us some tea in a very pretty pot, decorated with flowers and gilt leafing.

"Do you take milk and sugar?" he asked politely.

"Neither," I said with a smile.

The tea was something special, I could tell. It had a lighter color, something of green there too, and a softer flavor. He offered me biscuits which, he said, Mrs. Mounsey had baked herself. He then took a seat on a sofa under the window.

"You will have met, of course," the President said. "Gatsby is a kind of guest-of-honor, fought until the last minute. Mounsey is my right arm, my memory, and my organizer."

He stood with the cup and saucer in his hand, stepped to the window, turned to me with a smile.

"Quite a number of chaps you should look out for, Gatsby.

"We're lucky to have Captain Crosby from the American Expeditionary Force. He's going to be teaching, part of the SCR, helping us out, great fellow.

"One of your fellow undergraduates is Gerald Gent. I mention him because he signed up when he was technically still at school and rose to the rank of Lieutenant Colonel. Can you believe that? We have an undergraduate who was a Lieutenant Colonel until just a few months ago.

"You already know Norrington and Cusworth, fine men the two of them. Cusworth's father is pretty ill, I understand, so of course his son's life and future could change completely at any time. He's doing some kind of musical thing, jazz he calls it, not my cup of tea."

We were together, the three of us, for a further half hour or so. He and Mr. Mounsey talked a bit of college business: new students expected over the short time ahead before Easter, the improvement in funding, and the possibility of some kind of tribute to the fallen dead of Trinity College.

In my rooms, Cadman had replenished the small fire though this was no longer necessary. The weather had been temperate and a fuller and warm spring was expected.

I opened the President's gift-book once more, this time towards the end. Again it was Cicero:

"To me, indeed, my lords, death is now actually desirable, since I have discharged all the duties that have been committed to me and all that I have undertaken."

I knew nothing of this Roman. I had seen death in abundance, death in the discharge of duty. Thanks to heaven, and to whatever god, no such duty unto death would ever be invoked again – for anyone.

Chapter 5

In the dining hall that night, after the Latin grace, there were few men eating and I shared a table with Norrington, Cusworth, a quiet student called Anderson, and several others I did not know. At this and other times I was aware that my Trinity experience, while hospitably inclusive, also reinforced my sense of difference, my American identity, most of all my deep individual separateness.

The people and incidents were real enough – at the time. In another dimension I could have been living a dream. Accordingly some of the things I have written here may be more in the nature of a traveler's sketches than an account of scientific observation. If anyone were to attempt my story in the future I trust that the Oxford days will be short and modest in their telling if, even, believed at all.

At a separate table that night in Hall were half a dozen new arrivals, still schoolboys to my eyes, rather loud and determined to be excited. They broke and threw bread at each other and an older scout, in black waistcoat, plump stomach, and watch chain, marched with majesty up to them and advised them that there would be a fine for bread-throwing if they continued. He held before them a framed notice which read as follows:

"*Gentlemen coming from homes where Bread throwing at the dinner table is habitual and finding a difficulty in conforming suddenly to the unfamiliar ways of higher civilization, will be permitted to continue their domestic pastime, on a payment of 5/- a throw, during their first year, After that the charge will be doubled. RWR.*"

The food was simple but decent: lamb with cabbage

and a treacle pudding which also tasted rather welcomingly of brandy or whiskey.

"Don't forget the *Thirteen Club*, Gatsby," Norrington said, rising from the bench along the table. "It is Sassoon who'll be there, confirmed. Quite a controversial bloke, could be interesting. Anything I can do to help, just pop in. 'Night now."

"I'm off too, Gatters, old sport," Cusworth said, rising. "Let's make plans! Lots to do, eh! Good night, old sport."

I was tired, more tired than I could recall, other than on the long nights on the battlefield. The bed in my room was narrow, as small and squeezed as the barrack rooms I had been in during my earliest training, but the mattress was comfortable and Cadman had put some sort of bed warmer between the crisp and clean white sheets.

I shall not forget the seconds of relief, the downflow of pleasure that ran through me as I lifted the blankets on that first night in Trinity, slid down, grateful and sighing for the warm place that Cadman had manufactured, stretching myself down and down, and finally reposing my head on the pillow. *Oh you, English!*

I dreamed.

I do not know why I dreamed or why I should dream that I was, again, sailing across the oceans in search of... what? I imagine I was in search of Daisy. Yet there was no anxiety or haste. The ocean was blue and still and the sky was a pale turquoise, cloudless with an almost silver sun. Most of all there were the sirens who swam in the warm water, sirens like the siren I had thought to have seen at the lake in the London park – with the green light, mermaids, with silver tresses and silver tails, all smiling, gold-skinned, at peace with their world of beauty.

As far as I recall, I was alone in my dream on the sailing vessel. Though the wind was benign, the sails were full enough to move in steady elegance through these mermaid seas. I waved as I sailed by them, they returned the greetings, and, as I passed, I heard their siren songs, high wordless harmonies, which somehow strengthened rather than seduced. Then, boom!

"Eight o'clock!"

Cadman vigorously pulled open the curtains from my window.

"There's a kettle of hot water. The Dean wants to see you."

He walked out without another word.

I knew he had other "gentlemen" to attend to. I had used the chamber pot under the bed during the night, before the full depth of sleep, and thought it best to leave it. There was a large and ornate jug filled with cold water, standing in a similarly ornate bowl. Alongside these was a still-steam-from-the-spout kettle that Cadman had brought.

Pleased with the American Safety Razor Company's "Ever-Ready" which I took everywhere with me, I poured water from Cadman's kettle into the bowl, located a mirror from the study-room, and, with the bristled brush I had bought in New York, along with a stick of Ingram's shaving soap, I worked up a good lather and enjoyed my first shave in Trinity College – smiling to myself at this juxtaposition, having shaved on strict orders in the training camp at Beauregard, and now, a reader of Cicero, in the spires of English Oxford.

Much of what followed was typical of the days I spent in Trinity.

Cadman would wake me each morning with a firm statement of the time and an athletic opening of my bedroom curtains. He always brought a brown enamel kettle of hot water and always checked that the cold water jug was full and whether or not I had used the chamber pot.

In fact, embarrassment stopped me from using it after that first night. Lavatories were not far from my staircase and, even one night in unexpected and brief thunder and downpour, I preferred to scuttle to their hygienic efficiency rather than, as I felt, lower my status in Cadman's esteem. Our biologies are both friend and social foe.

I went into the Hall each morning for breakfast.

The food, again, was modest and, I suspected, sometimes a re-serving of what may have been a meal of the day before. Sometimes meat. Sometimes fish. Always with potatoes and bread. Yet somehow I felt that what was going on in the Trinity kitchens, places of pride and presentation, was part of some longer master plan, a determination that as the college grew back to posterity at least one manifestation of that return should be gastronomic – the other perhaps horticultural.

I did, as I had promised myself, on more than one occasion leave my bed in the middle of the night, listening first for a total silence, and then make my way to the lawns which were, as the moon grew anew, a place for dreams – of Daisy or even with the hint of siren songs far, far, far away in the flow of the River Thames, or the Isis as they called it here – some said for the goddess of wisdom and magic.

On those magic nights I would walk softly to the lawns and into the dark of their centers and if there was no rain and the air, by now, was warm, I would stretch out on the careful grass and watch only the sky. The scent of the gifted Trinity gardeners' work with shrubs and flowers touched my nostrils. Far away an owl would call to me but most of all it was the stars over Trinity lawns which dug themselves deep into my soul.

I have said before that this record is for me alone. I shall not reject my Oxford days but, for the life to come, I shall store them away safely in an archive of my own reflection, boast of them never and be touched only as memory will let me be touched. The pain which came later can never be forgotten.

Whenever Trinity was mentioned later, naturally the good souls I had met would ease into my mind: the Norringtons, the Cusworths, the Gents, the Andersons, the Crosbys, the Blakistons and the Highams, Madge and the musicians and all others I knew and who befriended me. Yet most of all I think it was probably the stars over the lawns at night which chiefly crowd the cells of memory. I am grateful for those moments always.

On that early morning at Trinity, with Cadman's brief time checking and after my shave and breakfast, I went to find the Dean who had asked to see me. He was known to all as Tommy Higham and was an altogether more relaxed and humorous man than the rather careful President – though equally earnest and likely to frown when he discussed his own plans for the college.

"I'm pleased to meet you, Gatsby," he said, offering a chair in his study. "I know pretty much about your war service, Argonne Forest, terrible, but what a victory! I was with General Milne in Salonika myself so I can have a sense of what it was like. I'm here to welcome you and, briefly, to suggest what you might like to study. Any ideas?"

"Hardly, sir. I haven't had much chance to explore academic matters – but I'm beginning to have a kind of appetite for books, you might say."

He laughed: "All books? Any books? Any old books?"

I was embarrassed and must have shown it.

"My own subject is classics, Gatsby, ancient history, Greek and Latin, that kind of thing. But I would like you to feel you're getting somewhere. So –"

He took a thin book from his desk and passed it to me.

"Virgil. A really popular poet in his own lifetime.

"This collection is called *The Eclogues* – don't worry about that, it just means *selections*. Take a quick look through them, Gatsby–there are ten poems all together. I'd like you to look at number four. A golden-age theme. Read it carefully. A few times. Would you mind doing that?"

"Of course not, but..."

"By next week I'd like you to write me an essay. Don't worry, it's just about what you think, not a test. Write an essay about Virgil's golden age and what you think about the world in 1919–post war, post battle, whatever you like."

"Sir, I really can't..."

"I've been closed in with young men for years, you know. Here and Salonika. I was with the Oxford and Bucks Light infantry. I'm not a prophet but I can feel certain that you are the kind of man who makes happen whatever it is he decides to make happen. Have a sherry."

"No thank you, sir."

"I said have a sherry, Gatsby."

Undeterred he took two small and narrow glasses from a bookcase, a fine-looking decanter and poured minuscule measures for each of us.

"Sip it. It's a fino. I've had it since, well, would you believe, 1899–it was my father's."

He raised the glass, saying nothing. We both drank together.

"Sorry if I seem a bit demanding. But there are changes of attitude I want to make sure occur in this college – even right through the university.

"The President may have told you about the goings on before the war. They're starting to call that the Edwardian Age, or the Edwardian Era, and I can't help thinking that some of the young men at that time thought they were god's gifts to the universe, demi-gods you might say.

"Vanity, conceit, exhibitionism – not all of them, of course, but it was not unusual to wreck the college lav-atories, break 'em up, and also their study furniture, to make bonfires in one of the quads, followed a while later by another in another quad and so on. The idea, thought to be funny at the time, was to keep the Dean running about like a mad horse.

"Many undergraduates of course are now, like yourself, older and wiser from military experience. I want to make it my job, though, that we move into a new age for Trinity, and for Oxford.

"Likely there'll be degrees for women next year, and it wouldn't surprise me if the college takes more Empire students too, even though the President and many others are doubtful about changing the Trinity tradition."

"What is that tradition, sir?" I had now finished my sherry with a total of eleven sips which it was sometimes my custom to count.

"Well," he hesitated. "We are very proud of the traditions of the college and the country.

"We are proud of all the men who have passed through our doors, and, of course, we are proud of the woman, Lady Elizabeth Pope, who was a foundress of our college.

"The public school tradition is something which the

British Empire must be grateful for. It has produced not only men of learning and wisdom, men of science and invention, but also men of courage and imagination who have fought, explored, taught, and given their lives to the furtherance of civilization over the past centuries.

"Trinity College stands strong and firm alongside that tradition, Gatsby, alongside those men, and that culture. For me that is something on which we must build across this new century.

"There may well, one day, be women and Africans in our rooms and in our tutorials. If so, let us hope that the Trinity of those distant days remains true and unashamed of its splendors of the past."

He laughed. He laughed loudly and cheerfully and rocked back in his swivel chair behind the desk.

"You have to forgive me, Gatsby, forgive the pomp and ceremony!

"I love the place, as will you. The President, believe me, is the finest man we could possibly have had during these past years. In Michaelmas Term, just gone, we were down to eleven undergraduates. Eleven! Yet over eight hundred fought and over a hundred were killed. Doctor Blakiston kept the college together, kept it functioning from day to day, and I was delighted to return here and take up some of the burden from his shoulders.

"Is there anything you would like to ask me, Gatsby?"

"If I am to study, to write essays and read, sir, how am I to get hold of the books I need?"

"Most undergraduates open an account with Mr. Blackwell, the bookshop next door, who has also incidentally let us have some land to work on to extend the college around Kettell Hall. Once you've gone through the matriculation ceremony there'll be no problem for books there. You are a Trinity man and Trinity men are trusted."

Only a few men at a time were matriculated in a ceremony of sorts in the Sheldonian Theatre. I had no chance to record everything in my note book but I recall that Cadman borrowed for me a short black gown and one of the square caps that some called mortar boards. Along with new arrivals I joined a procession into the Sheldonian where speeches and replies in Latin took place and where we, the new undergraduates, bowed our heads and mumbled knowingly.

I was later told that this ceremony, to include "guests" like myself, was unorthodox, somewhat improvised and unofficial, and was a special dispensation which had only been made for those who were coming to Oxford from the battlefields.

From the ceremonial event I crossed the Broad Street straight to Mr. Blackwell's shop and opened an account without questions. I found a book which I hoped would be helpful, still uneasy about what Dean Higham had told me to prepare.

The book was terrifyingly entitled: *Virgil's Messianic Eclogue, Its Meaning Occasion and Sources, by Joseph B Mayer, W. Warde Fowler, and R. S. Conway.*

I opened at the first verses of the poem which, again thank goodness, were in both Latin and in English. Neither made sense to me.

Muses to whom Sicilian shepherds sang,
Teach me a loftier strain. The hazel copse
And lowly tamarisk will not always please.

He had seen me, Tommy Higham said, as one who would persevere. If my oneness of spirit for Daisy Fay meant a oneness of spirit for Virgil too – then, very well, a challenge! – I would not fail to understand this writing somehow. In the week or so that followed, I read the Virgil poems many times and some of the feelings chimed with the task that Higham had set for me. In my private world, my own and inner golden age, there was, of course, the certainty of love and Daisy.

In the more general world, that of Oxford, of America, of Europe, and of 1919 and onwards, there was the dream of a destiny of peace and prosperity. Virgil's words were not too far removed:

"Come then, dear child, Jove's mighty heir,
Begin thy high career; the hour is sounding.
See how it shakes the vaulted firmament,
Earth and the spreading seas and depth of sky!
See, in the dawning of a new creation
the heart of all things living throbs with joy."

I wrote the best thing that I could, no more than four short pages, stirred by the truth-to-be of the dawning of a new creation, the end of all wars, an American and English golden time. Higham was kind and complimented me on writing from the depth, as he put it, of experience and insight.

Meanwhile other elements of Trinity life merged with my own.

I bought a bicycle for thirty shillings, second-hand, from Gardner's in Gloucester Green. It was a pre-war Humber from Coventry. I used it to ride to Woodstock and around the Cotswolds, alone and eager.

At such times two things occurred that warmed my spirits: people waved to me over fences and hedges in all the villages and meadows I passed and also the trust in Oxford itself was such that I frequently left the bicycle against the walls of the Broad Street overnight, and it was always there each morning. *Oh, you English!*

I took up cricket, bought a pair of well-cut white flannel pants, a special shirt, wide-collared and cool for the summer, and a white knitted woolen pullover with the colors and the crest of Trinity College incorporated into the pattern, white socks, and special shoes that were to be whitened with dampened coloring from a pad.

It was Tommy Norrington, as I learned to call him, who first showed me how to hold the bat.

"Two hands on the handle, steady and confident, thumbs pointing down, the flat side straight out front."

It was Gerald Gent, the former Lieutenant-Colonel who showed me how to bowl – on the long lawns of Trinity gardens.

"There's still underhand bowling," he said, "but if you take my word you'll do the overhand thing. Don't throw it or chuck it like you might do with a baseball. Watch me."

He took hold of the red leather ball, stepped back a few yards – six to ten I estimated – ran forward to what he had set down as "the crease", spun his right arm high into the air, negotiating (as it seemed to me) with his left arm across his face, and then let fly the ball like a cannon into the grass a few yards ahead, where it landed with a thud and dented the perfect Trinitarian turf.

We played what they called a "friendly" with a village team in Wolvercote, just outside the city and where we ate cheese and pickles and drank ale at a pub called *The Trout*. I scored seventeen runs, and was delighted that the cheers from the villagers, led by a Squire Thornton, but also from my fellows of Trinity, were a genuine tribute to this American playing the English national game for the first time.

It was Johnny Cusworth who seemed to value our friendship more than I could understand and most of all. I had to conclude that he was, simply, a man of easy and open charm such that this Yankee-soldier, who had fought and risked, merited his friendship. There were many rules, regulations, traditions and sillinesses about the Oxford life that I could not easily understand or follow. I mention this because on one weekend Cusworth suggested that we might "go out on the town" in London but must let nobody know because it was against the rules in term time.

"Not allowed to leave Oxford till the vacation," he said. "Unless you have a family problem or something. Which, by the way, could happen with my father."

We told no-one and from somewhere Cusworth borrowed a glorious white Prince Henry Austro-Daimler which he parked in St Giles so as not to be noticed by the college and which took us, one sunny Saturday afternoon, from Oxford to Mayfair. That is how I came to learn the foxtrot.

We drove for little more than an hour along the road and the signs showed that we were well on our way to approaching London.

"We'll stop for a bite, old sport, know a good place. Nice girl there too, you'll like her."

We turned off the main London road and drove for no more than ten minutes along a country lane.

We finally stopped at a pub and I may have gasped and smiled as Johnny parked the white Austro-Daimler in its forecourt.

If I had been shown a photograph or a sketch of this pub – called *The Moon and Fox*, by the way – I would have said at once that it was part of a Hollywood set for a movie about Queen Elizabeth the First, starring perhaps, with luck, Colleen Moore as a young lady-in-waiting or as a flighty country girl.

It had walls timbered with black beams and white plaster, a thatched roof which hung generously over those same walls, bow windows which were diamonded with lead and lensed in each small pane with what looked like the bottoms of bottles, glinting and grooved, and an ancient front door, now open, but studded with thick nails and bolts, ornamented with shining brasses of horse heads, moons, and foxes, and overhung with baskets of flowers in blue, red and orange.

We walked in to the polish-smelling bar, adorned in turn with shining brasses and ancient framed engravings of fox-hunts and squirely gentlemen with their ladies.

Behind the bar stood a young and smiling woman, exceptionally pretty and smart in a high-necked and frilled shirt with a black velvet ribbon at the neck, and – to my astonishment – virtually the twin sister of Colleen Moore herself.

"My goodness! My gracious!" she exclaimed with a huge smile when she saw Johnny. "The lord himself!"

She stepped from behind the bar and, open-armed, embraced him tightly. He lowered his head to kiss her gently on the forehead.

"Lovely, lovely to see you!" she said. "I was going to come over to Oxford myself and shake your cage!"

They hugged each other for a while.

"How is he?" Johnny then asked her.

"He's fine," she said in almost a whisper. "Just fine. He'll be starting to crawl any time. He's lovely."

"This is a good friend from Trinity," he extended an arm in my direction. "Jay Gatsby. He's from our colonies in

America. Brave fella, been fighting the Kaiser and nearly killed him. Anyway, the President has made him guest of honor and I thought I'd bring him round to say hello – bit of trout pie too, maybe, yes? That and your own cider?"

The young woman leaned forward to me in a gesture I could not at first make sense of. When she closed her eyes I understood that I was expected to kiss her on each cheek – which I did. She smelled of orchid. She smelled of Daisy.

"Gatters, this is Vicky. Victoria Braithwaite. May Queen and local swimming champ. The most gorgeous girl in Buckinghamshire. She owns this place, old sport, since her father died last March, and as you can see it's a heaven-on-earth. One day I'll coax her to London and she'll star at the Royal Command show."

Telling us that, strictly speaking we were far too late for lunch but of course in the circumstances she would make an exception, she showed us to a table by one of the bay windows with a view of green hills and a shining stream. She then brought us trout-pie and large glasses of pale cider. As she served these she slipped an envelope to Johnny.

"Just a photo," she said. "I thought you'd like it: Michael, when he was six months."

Cusworth took the picture from the envelope when she had left us. He looked at it for a moment and smiled, then placed it in an inside pocket and raised his cider glass.

"Here's to you, old sport. Hope you can meet a gal like Vicky some day. Bet you will."

We drank and ate in silence for a while.

"May I ask you a question?" I said uncertainly

"Please do."

"You call everyone 'old sport' – is that an English saying of some sort? Is it polite?"

He laughed and wiped his lips with a pale blue napkin.

"Don't tell a soul, Gatters, but I heard it once and it came to my rescue.

"You see, there are so many fellas on the estate that I could never remember their names. I got a bit embarrassed calling everyone Mr. Mumble so when I heard this rugger player call his captain 'old sport' I thought to myself, that's it! And I've used it ever since. Nobody's offended and the old memory cells get a decent break for a change. You should try it." I could never quite see that happening. With an American accent, surely, it would sound affected and pretentious.

We ate the lunch, and the chat was light-hearted enough with a little speculation from Johnny as to what the 1920s would bring.

"Jazz, and more jazz is my bet," he said. "That's why I'm doing the *Jazz à Spires*. We've seen the end of all wars, Gatters old sport, and the twenties will be the age of what they're already calling the flappers and the good times. Can't wait myself."

Before we got back into the automobile Cusworth excused himself and disappeared for a few minutes with Vicky.

"Let's go, old sport, London here we come!" He sprinted to the motor and started the engine with a shout of happiness.

We came into London along the same Bayswater Road where I had met Olman and seen the siren only a short time before. It felt very different now: with Johnny in the smart white car, the recent meeting with Vicky, and most of all with the men I now knew in Oxford and the money I already had to my account, I was, I felt at this time, the true Gatsby, the Gatsby for Daisy. The plan was working. Jimmy Gatz was a character for fiction or forgotten dust.

"We go down to Mayfair," he said. "It's a bit early but no harm. The hostesses will all be free and we can take our pick, what?"

We drew up in Berkeley Square – we pronounce it BAR-clay, he told me – and walked in the light sun through the trees of the square to a door which had in bold and brightly colored words the sign: THE BLUE GARDENIA.

"Good evening, m'lord" the doorman said, a young man with a black moustache and red burgundy uniform. He half saluted as Johnny walked past him. We were there for four hours or so. We drank little and danced even less.

Johnny was right about the hostesses. We were no sooner shown a table by the *maitre d'* (as Cusworth called him) than five or six girls of astounding good looks and fashion walked nonchalantly by the table. He whispered to me with a grin: "Just take your pick, Gatters, they're all smashers I can promise you."

"Why, hello, Rita... isn't it?" he said to one of the girls, dark and Hispanic, in a short red dress, headband and waving feathers.

"Hello!" she said with enthusiasm. "I remember you! February wasn't it? We had champagne!"

"Please join us," he said and the young lady, Rita, sat down.

"This is my friend Jay. He's from America. Just arrived. Thought I'd show him round."

"Ask Tanka to join us then," Rita said. "He'll like Tanka, and they'll get on like a house on fire."

Not waiting for an answer she stood up from the table, waved and called aloud: "Hey, Tanka. Come over here. Someone wants to meet you."

Tanka was tall and statuesque in a fitting dress which,

below the waist, said a kind of hello to the new girls' fashions of short and twitchy skirts with a silky fringe and tassels. She was Russian.

I had never been in a situation of this sort before and I had no idea what was expected of me. These young and exceptionally attractive women were called hostesses, but I could not begin to guess what this meant.

In fact it meant little.

Johnny ordered a magnum of the most expensive champagne that the Blue Gardenia possessed.

"If we don't finish it, take it home," he said to the girls with a smile.

I made a note later and I think the wine may have been Pol Roger, vintage 1892. It tasted good to me, but I realized that I had no notion of what made a good or bad wine. At times like this, and there were many during these days, it was *America-America* which whispered to me from within me – land of the free, the new and the young, the no-need-to boast, the land of the rich-with-pride.

Tanka explained that she had left Russia because of all the fighting. Her parents, she said, were aristocrats and cousins of the Tsar. She was working in this club because she needed money but also because she could trust young men like Graf Cusworth, as she called him. We talked, we danced a little – Tanka taught me the basic steps of the fox-trot – and I was thankful that Johnny was capable of animated and amusing conversation without tiring or exhaustion. He appeared to have anecdotes of a jokey and inoffensive kind on any topic, at any time, for anyone.

It was after ten when we decided to leave. Tanka gave me a printed card with her name and a telephone number.

"I can come to see you also, if you wish," she said. "It will not cost too much and will be my pleasure."

It was after midnight when we arrived back in Oxford and Johnny left the motor again in St Giles.

"We'll have to climb in, old sport. Got to be pretty careful though. Anyone sees us and they call the police."

New building works were going on close to Mr. Blackwell's bookshop and Kettell Hall inside the college. Cusworth seemed to know exactly what he was doing and by bending a bar here, moving a plank there, and climbing over some low scaffolding we were back in Trinity, where Cusworth put a finger to his lips.

"Quiet back to your set," he said. He put a hand on my shoulder. "You're a good man, Gatters old sport, and it was good to be with you. Join us for the jazz, what?"

In the dark he broke the rule about not crossing the front lawn and had soon disappeared. I went into the garden and lay down on the grass. A comet flew across the sky. Otherwise the stars were big and still, and I saw this as an American sky, the sort of sky the pioneers would know, the sort of sky that would have been seen by sailors' eyes when they marveled at the green breast of my own new world. I sat up.

"I am Jay Gatsby," I said clearly into the night. "I have a dream. I have the dream of America and the desserts of trust. I have love. I have time. I have Daisy. Og de levede lykkeligt til deres dages ende." The only Danish I had ever seen or knew.

I said this in the dining hall three days later and was told that I was to be sconced.

Earlier that day I had gone to have sherry with Madge

Wellesley in Somerville College. As she had warned, there was still the feel of a hospital about the place, but along with a few of the young men who remained, sometimes with crutches or eye-patches, arms in slings or no arms at all, there were several serious looking young ladies who seemed determined to wear spectacles and to carry a prominent pile of books.

Madge played me the jazz she had promised. She had a wonderful Columbia disc gramophone with a large amplifying horn and a selection of jazz records, some of which were new to me. She also gave me a sherry and offered some biscuits which she called macaroons.

It was a room overlooking the garden: a single room with desk, chairs, washing basin and a bed. We talked about the music for most of the time and she told me more about Johnny Cusworth and his musical affections.

"The performance in Trinity should be great fun," she said, "I'm looking forward to it."

Then she asked me what I intended to study. I explained that I'd written what I described as "a note" for the Dean about Virgil's poem.

"Literature and philosophy? And more of that?"

I shook my head.

"It sounds much more terrifying than it actually is," she said, and once again I was struck by her ease and amiability. "All Kant is trying to do, for instance, is just to try to help us work out what we *should* do. When an action is right. When it's brave and to be admired, or when it's done for effect, or what we should all do every time – a moral law in fact. Should everything we do be, as they say, open and above board?"

"What do you think?" I asked her.

"It's hard," she said thoughtfully. "We know that there are people who will die anonymously for a good cause, yet at the same time conceal their behavior from others when they think that is in their own interest."

"And lies – or falsehoods?"

"On the whole Kant would say that a lie is always a lie and that the truth, if known, should always be told."

"What do you think?" I said again.

"I am no Kant," she said with a smile, "I think he was right to examine, to analyze and make the attempt to define. The world we live in was not known to him."

"Would you lie to me?" I asked the question lightly, not meaning very much.

"No, I would not."

She paused, looked out, looked back at me, rose from the chair on the far side of the room, took off the gramophone record and replaced it with another, walked back to her chair, sat down, looked at me, she opened her mouth to speak, closed it again, turned to the window.

"Is not telling the truth the same as lying?" she asked.

My own situation, Gatz into Gatsby, North Dakota to Venice and Rome, unsurprisingly dominated my mind as she spoke.

"I think it is right to be creative..."

"With the truth?" she laughed, turning fully to me, eyes large with laughter through her lenses.

"All lives," I looked for the words to express my honesty of opinion, "all lives are surely a mix of fact – truth, if you like – and fiction, that's memory, imagination, hope and expectation, isn't that right?"

"But is *not to say* the equivalent of *saying false*?"

"I do not understand the question," I said. It was true

that I did not, nor did I understand the gravity with which she spoke it.

"Very well." She leaned forward towards me, intertwined the fingers of her hands together, looked firmly – that's the only word – into my eyes, then spoke. "I have fallen in love with you."

If we had been shooting for the Keystone Cops, in *The Bangville Police* say, I would have fallen over backwards from my chair, lain rocking with my feet kicking in the air, my eyes rolling like marbles and silent-movie prattle bursting from my lips. As it was, I simply dropped the little sherry glass and made to close my mouth after the jaw had fallen to its fullest range.

She laughed again, and it was in no way false. She laughed in the chair by the bright light of the window, and she laughed with her head tossed back and her red bobbed hair almost touching the pane.

"I'm afraid it's true," she said at last. "But please don't worry, Jay. I expect you already have a lady love. I also know that you will not be here for very long, but, even when we first met, there was something... something lasting about you that made me want to see you more. And the more I thought about you, the more I realized, well, that it was love, yes, really. Silly, I know, and sudden – but there it is."

She was asking for nothing as far as I could see. When I was leaving Somerville College she gave me books that she said I would "thoroughly enjoy", and "please keep them, take them home with you".

One was a translation from the French. It was called *Julie – the New Heloise*. Another was called *Wuthering Heights* – "a great love story" she said – and a third was *The Mill on the Floss*.

"Each in its way tells us something about love, devotion and honor," she said. "If you keep them, as I hope you will, just remember me a little when you read them."

By now the collection of books in my rooms in Trinity was beginning to grow. Books – they were already a small library and I knew that, whatever else occurred, I would take them into my new and richer life. Libraries after all are surely in their way a proof of respect and fortune.

Before dinner in hall that evening I looked quickly through one of the books she had given me, *Wuthering Heights*. There was also a short resumé in the preface and I was able to understand the immortal love of Heathcliff for Cathy.

There were candles on the table in Hall that evening. President Blakiston, with other fellows, including Tommy Higham and Captain Crosby, were on the high table. I was, yet again, impressed and moved by the beauty and the dignity of the place. Norrington, Gent and Cusworth were on my table. The meal began with a thin vegetable soup and was followed by what Cusworth assured me, without naming the species, was local game. I think I may have recognized rabbit.

At their invitation, because I had the habit of saying nothing or little and of remaining detached during the meals, I was persuaded to say what I had been doing that day. I mentioned nothing about Madge Wellesley's declaration but I did say that I had been reading *Wuthering Heights*.

"Tell us the story, old sport," Cusworth said. "Never read it, and never mean to."

I improvised as best I could, conjuring up the Yorkshire Moors, the ghost of Cathy, and the Earnshaws. However, invention got the better of me and I spun the story to say how Heathcliff and Cathy had finally escaped together, that she was not dead after all, and so, I concluded:

"Og de levede lykkeligt til deres dages ende."

"What was that you said, Gatters old sport?"

"Og de levede lykkeligt til deres dages ende," I repeated with a smile.

"Meaning?"

"They lived happily ever after. Chuck Deacon was a man I was with in France, a good friend in fact. His mother was Danish. He used that expression all the time, whenever we won a patch of the forest..."

"What was it again, Gatsby" The man who spoke this time was a red faced and aggressive new acquaintance, one who had once muttered when we queued for a beer: "You Yankees don't own the place, you know!"

"Please. Let's leave it," Norrington said, and I felt that somehow he was coming to my defense but for what I could not begin to understand.

"Tell us again, Gatsby. What was that froggy stuff you said just then?"

I repeated the Danish sentence.

"Sconce!" the red faced man shouted at the top of his voice. "I sconce Gatsby. Sconce, sconce, sconce!"

"What is happening?" I asked Norrington.

"Oh, it's childish stuff, you know. Old rules of the college. You're not supposed to say more than a couple of words in a foreign language, not while we're eating. Ask for cider."

Young Cadman approached our table, now in the white jacket of a table-server.

"You could appeal, of course," Norrington said. "Send a note in Latin or Ancient Greek up to the President, giving your reasons, and he might let you off."

"Let me off what?" I was, in ignorance and confusion, anxious about what was to happen.

"It's up to three pints of cider, Gatters," Cusworth explained. "Don't bother to appeal – unless you're really fluent. Bring the sconce mug, Cadders, Cotswold cider."

A few minutes later a massive silver and beautifully carved mug was placed in front of me.

"Take a swig, old sport, we'll do the rest. You'll have to pay of course but that's the rules."

I drank some of the cider which was rich with its apples and spice. The mug was then passed round the table. The red-faced "sconcer" grinned. His name, I recalled, was Wilson-Hughes.

"You don't quite rule the world yet, you see," he said.

Norrington and the others warned me about speaking more than five foreign words, mentioning young ladies' names, not wearing a gown, outrageous clothing, being more than five minutes late, and one or two other rules at college dinner which were punishable by sconcing.

I was never sconced again. I also avoided Wilson-Hughes as best I could. The following day the windows of my room were broken.

"That will be Balliol," Cadman said. He was right.

The day after that, late in the evening, a group of Trinity freshmen climbed the walls between the colleges and threw fireworks into Balliol. At the same time they sang:

Bloody Balliol
Bring out your white man
Bring out your black man
Jack Johnson says so
And he should know!

I kept myself apart from these incomprehensible

skirmishes. The black and white thing made me somewhat uncomfortable, as did the Ku Klux Klan which had started again in Georgia in 1915. I had fought with black Americans and many of them had died.

The windows were soon repaired. I had an invitation in my pigeon hole from Madge Wellesley to accompany her to the New Theatre in George Street to see a performance which might also be presented before King George at the Royal Command Performance in July.

I posted a note to her:

"Thank you. I would love to come. Should I wear a dinner jacket? If not, could I be sconced?"

Chapter 6

The night before we went to the New Theatre there was *The Thirteen Club* to which Norrington had kindly invited me. Siegfried Sassoon was to read us his paper on *A War of Words* with which they said he intended to bring together political reports, speeches, poetry and the truths about the Great War.

The genial Tommy Norrington came to my rooms just after breakfast that day to tell me a little about Sassoon.

"I expect you won't have heard of him yet in America," he said, "but he's very much in the news over here. I thought it would be useful for you to know – also we'll be having a bit of cricket with him on the lawns around tea time. He loves the game. Be there if you can, Gatsby.

"Otherwise? He's a hero, no exaggeration. He single-handed captured a German trench on the Hindenburg line – sixty Germans against him.

"But he's also deeply mistrusted since he published a pretty strong attack against the way the war was being run – it's called *Finished with the War- A Soldier's Declaration*. They argued he was mentally disturbed, but we were lucky because later on he was a patient at Somerville. He's a Cambridge man, by the way."

I thanked Norrington and felt he might be the person to ask about something which had puzzled me since I had arrived.

"What's that, Gatsby?"

"I understood that Isaac Newton was at Trinity here – but no-one ever mentions him to me. Was he disgraced or something?"

"Wrong Trinity, old man. Trinity Cambridge, Sir Isaac

– a lot of folk make the mistake. Perhaps see you for tea and cricket?"

The weather was perfect that morning. It would soon be the Easter vacation but most of the men I knew in Trinity thought they would stay in Oxford. The former military men especially felt they wanted to "settle in again", get used to the new life. Younger men, boys almost straight from school, were more likely to be going home to their parents. I would stay in Oxford and various gestures of hospitality had been made to me.

Good Friday, as I remember, would be on the eighteenth of April and so the day of Sassoon, and my Oxford walk, would have been a few days before that.

The day in question was a day of spring sun, stroking the vivid green of the grass on the Trinity lawns and spotting the leaves of the trees, the limes and firs and larches, which the softest of winds stirred only a little so that the birds – and by now I recognized a thrush, a blackbird, three sparrows, a blue tit, and a robin – did not fly but cruised gently on the light air, smiling perhaps – if birds can ever be said to smile.

Trinity was arranged in three main sections. I walked from the sunny garden and its quad through the first arch, which also led to the dining hall, the kitchens and into the Chapel Quad. These were the second part, where Cusworth's abundance of the modeled spires of Oxford was already in place. I recognized Tom Tower from Christ Church, the dome of the Radcliffe Camera, the steeple of St Mary's church, and the tower of Magdalen Tower (Maudlin as I had been advised to call it for no clear reason).

In this, the chapel quad, the large windows of the dining hall and the chapel were dominant. To one side, opposite

Hall, there were smaller rooms, or "sets", or "staircases" where I believe some of the military were still being housed. As I walked through this quad that spring morning, someone was playing the organ in the chapel. I quietly entered to listen. When the music was ended I saw that the player was Wilson-Hughes, as red-faced and aggressive as ever.

"Forgive my intrusion," I said. "That sounded so good. What was it may I ask?"

"Nothing that your sort could ever create or understand," he snapped.

"My sort? I do not follow you?"

"It was the Toccata and Fugue in D minor by Johann Sebastian Bach, Gatsby. Your lot will bring us the shimmy and the sham – or whatever you call it. The signs of decadence are already there. Money, that's all you lot think of.

"My family goes back in Wales and Scotland for over seven hundred years. Gatsby? I have a strong feeling you're a phony. I had the name Gatsby checked out – doesn't seem to exist."

He strode from the chapel. The fragments of my life and the compilation of my new self felt, for this moment, to be in pieces on the chapel floor. I sat in one of the pews. A face rose in memory – Daisy? No. This was the face of the dead, one I had nursed in the war. I had loved a friend, tried to save a life. There was nothing to fear: Gatsby I am, and Gatsby I shall always remain. I left the chapel reassured by my own determination.

The third section of Trinity that I now entered was the front quad. To the left the President's lodging and down one side, at the far left of the careful lawn, a newer row of rooms. Somewhere beyond these would be Mr. Blackwell's bookshop, the new area of land he had released to the college, and also Kettell Hall. To my right the walls of Balliol College, Trinity's foe though I never understood why.

I left the archway of the dark looming chapel tower and called into the lodge for my pigeon-hole messages. There was a card from the Junior Common Room which told me that *The Trinity Triflers* were to hold a small dance in the Kettell Hall Lecture Room, there would be a jazz band, refreshments – though no set supper – and tickets were 6/- each from Edgar Vaughan-Russell. Young ladies, of course, were very welcome.

I asked the porter if I could leave him the money for tickets. He said he could look after this for me with pleasure. I gave him four half crowns and a florin and, unnecessarily I thought, he wrote me a receipt which he also signed.

"Two tickets for the dance, Mr. Gatsby. All paid up and done, sir!"

"Thank you, Mr. Gillam," I said gratefully.

I stepped out into Broad Street.

The sun was casting oblique shadows across the road in Turl Street. The college to the left, I remembered, was Exeter and to the right Jesus. Perhaps I would visit them later. For now I turned to my left, walked past *The White Horse* pub where the Italian-looking lady from Abingdon was washing the windows, on past another pub, the King's Arms, and towards a street called Holywell.

This end of the Broad Street was choked with bicycles, several motors, a horse and cart (collecting old rubbish and clothes) and even a donkey-drawn carriage with a man dressed as a clown with three small children.

Did Gatsby here feel like an Oggsford man?

I had decided to take the walk in order to think that question.

These notes so far have been, and will remain as I have said, something of a sketch of the people and the events which occurred to me during my Oxford days. I did not particularly want to be "an Oxford man" – and yet I had to confess to myself as I walked peacefully that morning that the sense of immortality and repose of this city, its colleges and people, even after the disruptions of the war, made their indelible mark upon me. Gatsby was becoming a four-part man: the young and poor Jay digging for shell fish on Lake Superior; then Gatsby the soldier; now Gatsby the willing Oxford learner; and all of them to become Gatsby the wealthy lover and husband of Daisy, a Heathcliff from North Dakota returning, rich, to claim forever his own devoted Catherine Earnshaw.

It was the face of Chuck Deacon, however, that rose before me, sharp and unforgettable, as I entered Holywell.

Holywell was a narrow and congested road close to the Sheldonian Theatre and to the crumbling busts of what I now knew were Roman emperors. The street itself was, like most of the city's streets, loud and somewhat dirty. The houses on each side, which I took to be small and dark dwellings for the less well-to-do, had been worn and neglected by the war years. Doorsteps were sunken or broken. Front doors flaked and grimy. Sometimes where a window had been broken, crushed newspaper or cardboard had been placed as a temporary repair. Here and there, however, a new brightness was perceivable. Occasional doors were freshly painted with the colors of spring: prim- rose, rose red, green and sky blue. But these were few. I walked on, Chuck still with me.

Chuck Deacon. With me now, here, Oxford, England. He was the friend I had seen wounded in France, who had died in a pit and remained there unburied for two days before I was able to carry him away from the zone. It was the worst moment of my life in terms of human suffering. He was badly shot by German machine guns, losing half his face and with deep blows to the chest, bleeding profusely in that pit near the Argonne Forest. He died around noon. I talked with him and did what I could. I nursed him for his last hours.

We had met when introduced by a man whose name, I think, may have been Conway – Nick Conway perhaps of the twenty-eighth infantry – who had known him as a student. Deacon was destined to be with me in the sixteenth. His mother was Danish, his father originally from Ireland.

Chuck Deacon, originally Charles, was a devout catholic, owing to his father's own faith. He wore a cross at his neck along with his military identification and each night, even in the thick of bombardment, he methodically knelt as best he could, and prayed to the mother of god that the lives, including his own, should not be lost in vain. With Chuck Deacon alive in my mind I walked the length of Holywell to Longwall and at the High Street I turned towards Magdalen College and Magdalen Bridge.

I still could not forget how his face had appeared when I moved his body from the pit. It was a face of death tied with affection that would live with me forever. Faces matter so much. The face of Daisy was, at that time, the rising sun of my total future. The face of Chuck was the face of tender pain.

"We'll meet in a good bar I know in the Village," he used to say during breaks in the fighting. "It's at the Hotel Albert, Eleventh Street and University Place. You never know who you'll meet there. Mark Twain was there and, way back, so was Walt Whitman. We'll remember all this time together, Jay, and we'll never forget the friendship."

Chuck was in memory alive with me when I decided for the first time to take what they called a punt on to the river.

"How long, sir," I was asked as the huge pole was given to me.

"Ten minutes? Will that not be too long?"

"It's whatever you like, my friend."

I stood as advised at one end of the punt and pushed off with the pole. The low flat boat moved forward gracefully enough and I toyed with the fantasy that Chuck was in there with me, maybe Daisy too, and we were doing a kind of Venice gondola through the streams of Oggsford. I had gone no more than thirty yards, I would guess, when a rowing boat of some kind skimmed swiftly in my direction. I swung the pole vigorously to try to alter my course, but the punt was uncooperative, shook and wobbled in irritation (or so it seemed), and made me fall, arms wind-milling, into the river.

Happily, in one sense, the river was shallow so I decided to walk back on the river bed, pushing the punt before me with the redeemed pole inside it, back to where I had started. There was forgivable laughter on the bank as I stepped out.

"Not used to this," I tried to smile. "Machine guns maybe. Oxford punts, watch out!"

I changed in Trinity, having still some of the flannels bought before my travels with Dan Cody and the good trousers I had bought in The Strand, and I went out again. Along Turl Street, into the High Street, then to Christ Church and the Cathedral. In the dining hall one of the older college servants, rosy and plump like so many college servants and in a white jacket, observed me looking at the portraits and told me that the one "by the door there" is Charles Lutwidge Dodgson, "one of the finest mathematicians who ever lived and who also happened to write about Alice in Wonderland".

I had heard of neither and once again I was struck by what some of my fellow Americans might take for an extreme of English conceit – knowing all, having all, leading all: the assumption that the depth and spread of the British Empire made all things familiar to all the backward tribes on earth, including mine. And yet... I was to learn later that our own Jack London, like Gatsby allegedly from San Francisco, had written *The Cruise of the Snark* from a book by this man, Dodgson, and the book dealt with travels that the young Jimmy Gatz might well have shared.

From Christ Church College I walked back to the junction called Carfax, and from there along the crowded and noisy Cornmarket to St Giles. As it was now after twelve o'clock I realized that the restrictive licensing laws of England would allow me to take a drink in the Randolph Hotel and it was there that a cheerful young barman who said "my name's Jack" gave me a my first half pint of Irish stout.

"If you never tried it, sir, you never lived."

It was, to my taste, thick, black and sweet and I wondered whether my appetite would ever recover from the experience. *The Randolph* itself was a cozy, informal and welcoming place. People from the city in their work clothes chatted together in the bars. Young couples sat smiling to each other at the corner tables. Older people, clearly not rich, sat with their pints or their gins, happy for a place of company and courtesy, still and untroubled.

From there I looked into the Ashmolean Museum opposite the hotel, spending almost an hour among the sculptures and the paintings. Once again, this European heritage as a thing not of trans-Atlantic conjecture but of the here and now was brought home to me. It made me feel deeply New World and American, alive for the Dream, not for the past but for the future, and the future only.

I stopped at *The Bird and Baby* for a fruit juice and fish cake, then on further to the Radcliffe Infirmary and Somerville College.

Back in Trinity I discovered that the man Sassoon had now arrived and was with Norrington, Cusworth and others, practicing cricket strokes in the garden. I went there to watch and was glad that no-one paid attention to me as I sat on the grass some distance away. Detached observation was something with which I had always felt comfortable and it grew deeper each day in Oxford.

After watching the cricket it was time to dress for the club reading.

By now I had bought new clothes and many new books, including work by John Stoddart whose lectures had been recommended to me by Mr. Balfour, and my wardrobe, including also several bright new shirts which I liked especially, now also contained what was referred to as "black tie". This meant a black jacket with silk lapels, black trousers with a silk seam down the leg, a black double-buttoned waistcoat, a stiffly starched winged collar and – finally – a black tied bow.

The *Thirteen Club* was meeting in Cusworth's rooms on Staircase thirteen in the Garden Quad. There were more than thirteen there and I realized that undergraduates from other colleges had been invited as guests, as I had myself.

A young man I had not met before and who told me that he was from Exeter College was on the seat next to me.

"Sassoon is a miracle – and a signpost," he whispered.

There was, it is true, something striking and trustworthy about Sassoon's looks. He sat before us in a very simple jacket and flannels. It was one of the college fellows, Harold Pritchard, who spoke first and introduced Sassoon, with words which were neither laudatory nor critical. He simply said that Sassoon had been decorated for bravery and that his opinions and his poetry were a matter of increasing general knowledge. I made such furtive notes as I could of what followed, watched with a kind of sympathy by the Exeter man next to me as I scribbled.

"Words and war are what I'd like to talk about," Sassoon began. "I should like to start, if this does not seem too vain, by reading you a verse from one of the poems I had published earlier this year – in the *Cambridge Magazine* as it happens…"

There was a small rumble of laughter, more for politeness than hilarity.

"I called the poem *A Last Word*. May I read to you a verse from the second part?

"*'If I'd refused to fight, if I had done*
'Two years hard labour, four years on the rack,
'Instead of serving on the Western Front,
'You'd meet me with contempt; you'd think of me
'As an unspeakable blighter…'"

He read more and I was impressed by his calm matter-of-factness. He had a young and open face, despite all that must have happened to him and, reading, he raised his eyes the whole time to speak to us directly, face to face, eye to eye. It was an alert look of truth and candor.

After the poem he read what, he explained, he had written as Lieutenant Sassoon of the Royal Welsh Fusiliers and which had been published in the press in July 1917. I took notes again:

"*I am making this statement as an act of willful defiance of military authority because I believe that the war is being deliberately prolonged by those who have the power to end it,*" he began, and continued:

"*I have seen and endured the sufferings of the troops and I can no longer be a party to prolong these sufferings for ends which I believe to be evil and unjust. I am not protesting against the conduct of the war, but against the political errors and insincerities for which the fighting men are being sac*rificed."

He then read the paper he had prepared for us, reading further poems by one he described as a dear friend and comrade, a Welshman called Owen who had died, and he then extended his ideas to what he called the articulacy of violence: words as deception and words as revelation.

The reading of his paper lasted almost an hour. We listened in silence. There was no applause – it was not that kind of society. There was much nodding of heads, though two men walked out of the room without a word.

Decanters of port were then produced with the usual crystal glasses. I rose to approach Sassoon, merely to say how much I had enjoyed his reading, but the Exeter man laid a hand on my arm.

"Were you in the war?"

I told him I was, briefly describing the units I had been with, the men I had known, Chuck Deacon in particular, and the final battle I had been involved in.

"I was there too," he said, meaning simply that he had been in the war. "It's hard to settle back, don't you find?

I'm at Exeter now, reading English. The name's Coghill – I've a feeling the poems about this war will endure, don't you think? The '*War Poets*', can't you just see it?"

Coghill was rather grave in manner, serious, and gentle in speech, with almost a lisping mannerism which somehow enhanced his words.

"How about you? A Trinity man, I expect. What have you come to read?"

I explained that I had been offered a stay in Oxford as a gesture to American soldiers who had fought.

"I seem to have gotten involved with Latin poetry, philosophy and literature," I said.

"Could be worse," Coghill told me, "it's stuff that lasts a lifetime – shapes the way you think, and the way you behave, I suppose."

It was this man, Nevill Coghill, who introduced me to Siegfried Sassoon. The conversation was very brief.

"I saw you watching the cricket," Sassoon said to me, "but sadly you didn't join in."

"Not quite there yet," I said with a full Dakota accent by way of explanation.

"There's more to it than it seems," Sassoon replied. "Not as hectic as some of the sports in America obviously, and pretty tame compared with bull-fighting. I've always loved cricket – and in a way it's reflective of life itself – with the stillnesses, the boredoms even, and then the sudden sharp drama."

He went off and those of us left in the room chatted for a while, the sense on the whole being that Sassoon's view had some merit but several of the men declared that it would be wrong to do anything other than to honor those who had died in battle, of all sides and of all nationalities.

That night I returned to the garden once more when everyone else in Trinity was deeply asleep. There were clouds that night so that I saw nothing of the moon and stars, but a good wind stirred the trees around the periphery of the Trinity lawn, as I stretched out in my dressing gown on the grass. Behind me were the gate and the squared staircases of the Garden Quad. All lights were out. There was the smell of an evolving year, the latency of spring-into-summer, and as usual I checked who and what I was after the day just spent.

Oxford was making its mark on me, a mark which I would wish to conceal without shame or disloyalty. The Trinity people, and those like Coghill from elsewhere and soldiers too, had returned to a world of ancient customs and certainties where young Americans like myself, with no ivy-league tradition or parental status, would forever be in exile. It was not unlike the voyages I had made with Cody years before, a sighting of alternatives and even of a settled beauty, but such as would have to be left behind, and if not eradicated, then at least played down or made little of.

Have many made my journey? I wondered.

More of an American voyage, I concluded, than an English excursion. The English – or so it seemed in this first year after war – knew who they were and where they belonged. The girl at the station refreshment room, for example, would never become, or even wish to be, within the citadel walls of the University of Oxford. I guessed also that a man like Wilson-Hughes, proud in his contempt, would never have such young ladies in his circle. Yet the big-hearted, jocular and self-effacing Johnny Cusworth was (if my reluctant suppositions were correct) the father of a child with the young woman at *The Moon and Fox*. To generalize therefore was to fail to understand. The totality of this tapestry of England was not easy to comprehend.

There – on the Trinity lawn in the darkness of an Oxford night – I let Daisy spin towards me. We danced and we kissed, I smelled her delicious perfume and the cool moisture of her lips, and I pushed the calendar a year or more ahead to the time when we would be married, opulent with a place of our own at Louisville, with roadsters galore and foxtrots to the moon.

Perhaps it was Sassoon's talk that night which also and again brought the dead face of Chuck to my mind. Looking up to the clouded sky of night I saw his face once more, alive and dying. I wished no disloyalty to him but, as with turning the pages of a book, I folded him over to make place again for Daisy and for our sacred future.

Did I hallucinate? Or did I fall asleep momentarily and dream? Whatever the explanation, as I lay there on the lawn, to my right in the place behind the President's garden, a shimmering light appeared, shapeless at first but then, in silver, the walking image of the siren I had seen by the green light at the lake in London. She wavered and seemed to wave at me, then she sang. She was there for no more than two minutes but I felt the cold of the night air envelop me. As she floated away into the trees behind the wall I stood up to see. There were no signs. I returned to my room.

Madge Wellesley had suggested we should meet at a pub in the Cornmarket before going on to the New Theatre. It was old and cobbled, bow windowed, and lit with candles inside and an unnecessary fire of logs and twigs. She was no longer in blue stockings and did not wear her spectacles. For the first time I saw that she was wearing lipstick, rouge and eye shadow of a subtle blue. Her dress was surprisingly modern, tasseled with fringes and with pointed silk shoulder pieces. She also wore a cloche hat over her neat red hair. I wore the black dinner suit and tie, preferring mentally to call it a Tuxedo from the times I had heard it referred to for the smart set of Tuxedo Park.

She ate a plate of cockles and drank Irish Guinness.

"Did you get the Kant?" she asked at one point in our conversation, wiping a cockle drizzle from her lips and raising the dark stout to drink.

"I did," and it was true. Blackwell's bookshop had become a daily date for me, but I could not say why. Books and books and more books seemed a necessity, especially as things which I would want to take back home with me, to collect and to keep, to make a library that Daisy and I would share together. Many of the books, however, I confess had not yet had the pages cut where appropriate.

"I also got *Tom Jones* and *Tristram Shandy*." I felt a little pretentious in the telling. Madge nodded as if I had bought soap and a necktie.

"You'll find them useful," she said.

At the New Theatre in George Street there was what the English call variety, not unlike our Vaudeville or what Stan on the *SS Bardic* had called a concert party, but with performers who were billed as being "likely to be before the King at the Command Performance in July 1919".

The audience was the same mix as I had found on the streets of Oxford. The well-to-do in evening clothes, chiefly in seats or boxes at the ground floor level or the circle. Above them, less elegant perhaps but the women equally buoyant in boas, and hats and scarves and flowers, the men in shining bowler hats, white suits and embroidered waistcoats, were the majority. Some, however, were clearly poorer in thick wool jackets over curling collar shirts, with oiled hair and well-worn caps. While Madge and I were on the front row of the stalls, these were sitting in what they call "the gods", high above us, cheery and loud.

In the program there was a printed slip to tell us that "sadly Miss Ida Adams will be unable to appear but we are delighted to welcome Miss Binnie Hale from the original cast of *Houp La!* to take her place with the Hawaiian number, *Oh! How She Could Yacki Hacki Wicki Wacki Woo.* It was indeed the lovely girl from The Strand café I had met not long before.

The "star" of the evening, however, was a sturdy and assured Scotsman. I knew he was Scots from the outset by the kilt, the cap ("What do you call it?" I whispered to Madge. "A Tam O'Shanter," she whispered back to me, "I think.") and the strong tones of Scotland in his voice. Clearly the audience loved him and they rose to applaud at his first entrance. He sang many songs, each one cheered loudly by the crowd. I noted *Roamin' in the Gloamin'*, and *I Love a Lassie* but it was at the end of the performance that something happened which was so poignant and personal that I shall never choose to tell of it – other than in these pages which are to be closed forever.

At a break in his songs, Mr. Lauder waved down the standing and cheering crowd. It took several minutes to silence them. He smiled as they cheered but he clearly wanted to speak. "Thank yee. Thank yee!" He repeated. At last there was silence. He stepped forward.

"My last song tonight," he said (and I make no effort here to catch his splendid accent), "is one I've specially written myself. Some of you may know that my son, John, served as captain in the Argyll and Sutherland Highlanders. You may also know by now that he was killed in action. I have written this song for him."

The audience were all seated again now. They clapped respectfully with murmurs of sympathy.

"I should like it very much," he said, "if any serving soldier from this audience would kindly step on to this stage to join me in the song for my son – for his own fellow-in-arms. Please step up."

Madge grabbed my arm, smiling but determined, and she raised it, hissing to me good-humouredly: "You just have to do this, Jay. You were called to do it! Please!" Then she shouted up to Harry Lauder across the footlights: "Here's your man!"

She stood up, grabbed my arms and pulled me to my feet. I feebly shook my head but she was now laughing and gay, pushing me towards the wooden steps that led on to the stage. Mr. Lauder leaned towards me over the footlights and the orchestra pit, holding out an arm of friendship and welcome. I had no choice.

Onstage all the lights were upon me and I could see no further than the first six rows of the stalls. Madge was there, grinning, miming applause and blowing kisses with an outstretched arm.

"Where you from, son?" Harry Lauder asked me.

"I'm American."

"An' I'm a Scot, laddie, we can show these English, eh? What's your name?"

"Gatsby, I said. "Jay Gatsby."

"Well, Jay Gatsby, we're goin' to sing a song together. I'll sing it first so you get the idea – then together, yes?"

I nodded.

He waved to the conductor in the orchestra pit and the music started. He said, once more:

"For my son, John – John – "

Then the first verse, slow and contained, gentle yet firm, afterwards a chorus and he nodded to me as he sang it:

Keep right on to the end of the road
Keep right on to the end
Tho' the way be long, let your heart be strong
Keep right on to the end
Tho' you're tired and weary still journey on,
Till you come to your happy abode
Where all you love, you've been dreaming of
Will be there, at the end of the road.

He sang another verse, then this same chorus and he took my hand. By compulsion I felt that I must sing too, and I did – hopelessly, tunelessly in an accent which no linguist would ever be able to define. He sang the chorus again. Once more I did my best, this time the knowledge of Daisy and our future chimed for me with the final words, "till you come to your happy abode, where all you love, you've been dreaming of will be there, at the end of the road."

Mr. Lauder then called out to the audience:

"Ladies and gentlemen, the young lad wi' me here is called Jay Gatsby, and he's from the United States of America, and he came over to fight for us – and to fight wie us! Please gie a cheer to young Gatsby!"

They cheered, and some shouted enthusiastically: "Gatsby! Gatsby!"

We sang the song twice more, these times the entire audience were on their feet and I saw that all divisions of rank and splendor were dissolved. Ancient bearded men in "the gods" with torn coats and battered shirts, alongside their wives and children from the Victorian age, stood to sing with the jeweled ladies in the boxes and the smart young women with ostrich feathers and dangling necklaces. Young men still in uniform, arms in slings, or eyes patched, stood to sing with their mothers in dark silk dresses. I stood with Harry Lauder and sang. He slapped me warmly on the back, wished me 'good luck, son', and I noticed that Madge had dabbed her eyes to protect her makeup.

I walked with her back to Somerville and thanked her for a gorgeous evening.

"You can see why I have fallen in love with you," she said, matter-of-fact. "You are so extraordinarily human!" She kissed me lightly on the cheek and disappeared.

There was a letter waiting for me from Daisy in my pigeon-hole. I decided to relish the reading of it in the morning after sleep.

Chapter 7

The letter from Daisy was short. It was of no more than six lines but I counted the word "love" no less than eight times. Something in the tone and brevity made me consider, I think for the first time, that my days remaining in Trinity should not be too many. My virtual conscription to the college had been agreeable enough and I was grateful for the new experiences which had abounded. However, I felt that my absence from Daisy, and from the firm future of my existence with her, should not be prolonged. As always she said that she was missing me. The phrase comes readily to lovers' pens and lovers' lips, yet in this latest brief note I felt that the strength of the phrase, *missing you*, was apparent. I should not linger too long.

Easter Sunday fell on the twentieth of April, a day of summer sunshine and still air. I tried my luck with a punt once more, alone for self-respect, and was able to navigate a good half mile through the muddy and reeded waters of the Cherwell. My days and weeks were now, almost chaotically, filled with events and experiences which whenever possible I took care to mark, often dated, in my pocket note book – which is also how I know precisely that Daisy used the word *love* eight times in the short letter I have mentioned.

During the vacation, on Wednesday the twenty-third of April, there was a further meeting of *The Thirteen Club* and, thanks to the amiable Norrrington, I was once more a guest. The topic was simply: English poetry. The speaker was Sir Arthur Quiller Couch, a Cornishman (I was told) who was now in middle age and mainly in Cambridge but at home here in Trinity. He had thick dark hair and a flourishing moustache. He read from his own published anthology of English verse which was dedicated, I saw, to "*The President, Fellows and Scholars of Trinity College Oxford: a House of Learning, Ancient, Liberal Humane and my most kindly nurse.*"

"Anyone care to read?" he said at one point, and the uninhibited Johnny Cusworth stepped forward.

"Somewhere in there is a poem by William Morris," Cusworth said, "It's called *Love is Enough* and I've read it to one or two ladies once or twice."

Some of the *Thirteeners* chuckled.

"Yes, here we are!" Cusworth cleared his throat and began to read. For reasons which will become clear I later copied the poem into my own notebook:

"*Love is enough: though the World be a-waning,*
'And the woods have no voice but the voice of complaining,
'Though the sky be too dark for dim eyes to discover
'The gold-cups and daisies fair blooming thereunder,
'Though the hills be held shadows, and the sea a dark wonder,
'And this day draw a veil over all deeds pass'd over,
'Yet their hands shall not tremble, their feet shall not falter;
'The void shall not weary, the fear shall not alter
'These lips and these eyes of the loved and the lover.'"

It was childish or naive perhaps, but I changed for my own purposes the third and fourth lines of the verse and copied them out again, neatly and separately:

Though the sky be too dark for dim eyes to discover
The gold hat and Daisy fair blooming thereunder.

I continued in the days that followed to write one or two essays, if they deserve that title, for Tommy Higham and also did some literature under the guidance of Mr. Stuart Jones. I bought even more books, sometimes from the secondhand shops in the High Street as well as from Mr. Blackwell's so that the shelves in my study were soon full to overflowing with piles stacked together on the floor. These now included more major American works such as Melville's *Moby-Dick*, Twain's *Adventures of Huckleberry Finn*, Emerson's *Essay* and *The Conduct of Life*, and importantly Walt Whitman's *Leaves of Grass* – he would have been one hundred years old this spring, I noted. One quote of Whitman, which I valued especially, was placed on my wall above my desk:

"Oh while I live, to be the ruler of life, not a slave,
to meet life as a powerful conqueror,
and nothing exterior to me will ever take command of me."

All these books, I affirmed to myself in the optimism which still persisted at that time, would be with me in my home with Daisy.

There was also the small dance I have mentioned in the college itself for which I had already bought tickets from the porter. It was in the Kettell Hall lecture room and organized by a group of undergraduates calling themselves *The Trinity Triflers*. Madge Wellesley came as my partner in yet another and new fringed and shimmering dress, this time emerald green and with feathers to match in her gold hair band. There were only sixty of us, thirty couples, and the cost was six shillings each.

The place was small and somewhat confined but prettily decorated with Chinese lanterns and flowers. There was also a student jazz-band who played well and enthusiastically. We danced to *The Black Bottom* and, of all people, it was Johnny Cusworth who gave me the instructions which, he said, a young lady had taught him in New Orleans.

"I haven't the foggiest idea what it means, old sport," he said, "but this is what she told me, in these words:

"*Hop down front then doodle back. Mooch to your left then mooch to the right. Hands on your hips and do the mess-around.*

"*Break a leg until you're near the ground* (break-a-leg is a hobbling step, old sport, Cusworth explained), *now that's the Old Black Bottom Dance.*

"I know Madge'll have it right in no time."

He was right. She danced well and learned quickly. She also sang with the band, and I shall not forget her being slowly and gently smiling, turning to laughter between the two of us, with *A Good Man is Hard To Find:*

So if your man is nice,
You better take my advice
And hug him in the morning,
Kiss him every night,
Give him plenty loving,
And treat him right
For a good man now day's is hard to find.

Later in the evening we danced the Charleston together. She taught me the steps and the kicks and I did my best. When it was all over and we were both flushed with the music, the dancing and a kind of happiness, I walked with her back to Somerville, having agreed with the night porter, Hastings, that he would let me back into the college after my gallant duty with the lady. He was reluctant at first, as the college rules were very strict in such matters, but perhaps my being American and chivalrous persuaded him that my treble knock on the window of the lodge would allow him to open to me.

At the entrance to Somerville we said goodnight. Madge held out a hand which I, in confusion, shook formally. She said we should meet again, if only once or twice more, something spectacular perhaps, and added that she could feel I was soon to leave Oxford.

On other days there were smoking concerts in Trinity though these were now rare and were a leftover from the days before the war. They allowed us to smoke cigars, pipes or even cigarettes while musicians, chiefly recruited from among the undergraduates, played classical pieces or compositions of their own.

There were more feuds with Balliol College and these remained incomprehensible to me but I was pleased that my windows, easy targets, were not broken. I became more closely acquainted with fellow-freshman Gerald Gent who had reached the rank of Lieutenant Colonel while in the military and had also shown me how to bowl at cricket. We had enjoyable meals and conversations together in country restaurants and pubs outside the city, often overlooking the river and smooth-gliding swans.

Most of all it was the pile of books in my study, and a visit to Merton College, which gave me an idea of which I remain quite proud. Books were the source of it. There had been a note from Cecil Parke to visit him, at my convenience, in Merton College library.

"Ah, Major Gatsby," he said, rising from an armchair surrounded by bookshelves. "Just to let you know. Things are going extremely well for our projects in America and I shall be leaving in the next few days to take up my position there permanently. Scotch?"

He produced a bottle. I accepted a small measure with water.

"That your name has worked wonders is all I can say. Trust is so important, is it not? The suggestion is that you become entirely your own man at the start of next year, 1920. What you do after that with the considerable funds and bonds, plus shares in investments which will then be yours to draw at your own discretion, is up to you.

"Drugstores, or alternative markets once the prohibition laws are in effect, it is for you to decide. Mr. Wolfshiem remains the effective head of business, but you will be answerable to nobody but yourself from next year. You will have an extraordinarily large base of capital to start from.

"I just wanted to wish you all the best, as I shall be leaving. Here is my card with contacts in America. Sometimes I shall be in what our colleagues there rather affectionately call "hick towns" – that is to say, *not* New York, but you'll always be able to leave messages. All the very best to you, major."

He shook my hand warmly. In something like awe I observed the array of books in the Merton library. This confirmed my earlier intention and, once back in Trinity, I hurried to see Mr. Mounsey, the President's personal assistant.

"Would it be possible for me to see the President, sir?" I asked him.

He excused himself with a slight bow and left the room, returning almost at once.

"He has about half an hour free in his diary, Mr. Gatsby, so he could see you now if you wish."

The President, owlish still behind his rimless spectacles and as ever attired in first-decade clothes, waved me politely to a seat.

"Leaving us, Gatsby? Is that the point?"

"Well not quite yet, sir, though that may have to be considered." I stumbled with the words. "Family matters over in America," I improvised. He nodded.

"Then how can I help you, Gatsby?"

"I trust this will not sound impertinent, sir, but I have a suggestion to make – about the college."

He said nothing.

"You mentioned the enormous number of Trinity people involved with the war, sir, including those who died or were wounded."

"Quite so, Gatsby. What of it?"

"As I said earlier, sir, I have some considerable sums waiting for me in America. I also have the feeling, sir, that you would like to honor the Trinitarians of the Great War."

Again he just stared at me without speaking.

"Please forgive me for being so forward..." I hesitated.

"Continue, Gatsby."

"If it may be done anonymously, sir, anonymously now and for always, I should like to make a gift to the college of a thousand pounds."

"That is most generous, Gatsby, thank you."

"But – and again forgive me, sir – on condition that it is used towards the construction of a library in the college for the use of all present and future Trinitarians, a kind of War Memorial Library, sir."

He rose from his seat, walked round the desk and shook my hand. He smiled more broadly than I had ever seen him smile.

"You are a remarkable man, Gatsby, and no mistake. Remarkable. One could almost say clairvoyant. Thank you. I have pleasure in accepting your generosity and shall ensure that nobody – nobody ever, except for you and me – knows about this conversation or about your gift."

It was a good feeling, I have to say. The first time that I had ever played the role of benefactor of any kind, but confident that as my fortunes grew it would be one that I would enjoy to repeat. A new home for my father? Without question.

Preparations were now being finalized for the *Jazz à Spires* celebration.

Up to a third of the chapel quad was ornamented with the models of spires, domes, towers and steeples of the city and the university. I admired it in particular one afternoon when I was on my way to cricket practice in the garden, comfortable in my white flannels and the Trinity blazer which I now wore for all such occasions.

"Nothing like that where you come from, Gatsby, eh?" It was Wilson-Hughes also dressed for cricket, red-faced and lip curled in a way that I thought he must practice frequently when alone.

"It looks splendid, old sport!" I said, straight-faced.

"Old sport? Why you – "

At that moment Johnny Cusworth joined us, along with Tommy Norrington, J.B. Anderson, and two men from St. John's who would also be playing with the *Jazz à Spires*: Henry Vennick and Tom Ewan, now also in their college blazers and whites.

"Take a photograph, would you, Cadders, old sport," Cusworth said, holding out a Box Brownie as Cadman was making his way towards Hall.

"Certainly, my lord," Cadman said, and with swift efficiency had us lined up, myself to Cusworth's right, under the chapel arch and with the jazz set of model spires for our background.

"Another for luck, Cadders," Cusworth asked politely and Cadman obliged.

"I'll stick the prints in your pigeon holes on Friday," Cusworth told us.

Later that week I found an elegantly wrapped bottle of vintage champagne on the desk of my study. There was a short note from Madge, "For us to share, Saturday night."

"It came by special delivery," Cadman explained as he closed the curtains of my rooms.

"Thank you, Cadman. May I ask you something?"

"Within reason, sir."

Once again I had the slight impression he was standing to attention. I hesitated. My American ambivalence to the ways of the old world, the suspicion that I should simply know some things and ask no questions, forced me to think carefully before speaking.

"The other day, when you took the photograph – why did you call Cusworth "my lord", Cadman?"

"As you well know, Mr. Gatsby," he said as if reciting a well known declaration, "he is the son of the Earl of Doncaster, and in his own right he has the courtesy title of Viscount Cusworth, or Lord Cusworth. Therefore I call him, my lord, my lord – I mean, I call him my lord, sir."

"I did not know that, Cadman. Thank you."

"His father is also very sick, I understand, and may not, I regret to say, be alive when his son takes his finals."

Somehow I was again impressed: *oh, you English!* Nothing vain or pompous after all about this cheerful young man who would soon no doubt be the Earl of Doncaster. Frivolously I thought for a moment that Earl Cusworth would be a fine name back home for a black jazz musician.

Some days before the evening which got me into trouble with Madge, we had also spent the night together, with about twenty-three other undergraduates, on the banks of the River Cherwell. We had punts and wine and baskets of food, one or two guitars and harmonicas, and made small fires to roast – extremely badly – sausages and steaks.

We softly sang English and Scottish folksongs (which I did not know but which I was taught that night), played word games, dozed a little, held hands, some even swam in the muddy waters of the river. As daylight began to show we climbed back into the punts and slowly and smoothly moved down to Magdalen Bridge. For a long period of time nobody spoke. I heard birds: ducks and a heron and the sky birds of the spring. Then, as if by magic and from nowhere, the soft and haunting voices of a choir filled the air: so far, so far away, but through the lock of our attentions so near and so complete. I had never before heard any sound quite like it, not even the siren songs. I have certainly never heard any sound like it since. Madge held my hand and rested her head against my shoulder. Some two hundred or more young people, with older people on the bridge, switched everything off in their minds to hear the pure sound of these young boys, singing in the May morning from the very top of Magdalen Tower. Their voices carried beautifully, just as the sunrise birds had carried earlier, linking our human song to that of nature.

When it was over, we did not speak too soon or too easily. Madge suggested breakfast and I nodded. We found a place in the market and I ate eggs with bacon, thick bread with marmalade, and an abundance of strong brown tea (with milk!)

Madge arrived in my rooms for our private champagne party, just for two, in the early evening that Saturday. She was in a plain scholar's dress again, spectacles and blue stockings.

"Listen carefully. There is something very, very special," she said, "before you go home to the Statue of Liberty."

She explained briefly, at first I could not understand why, about the Queen's Own Oxfordshire Hussars who went to war in 1914 and were only now coming home.

There were also, she told me, only sixty-six soldiers left, after the war, from the Second Battalion of the Oxford and Buckinghamshire Light Infantry – which was, as I recalled, Tommy Higham's regiment.

Madge explained that, along with others in the county, the Duke of Marlborough, as also the Lord Lieutenant of Oxfordshire, was giving a special ball, a huge affair, with entertainment and reception at Blenheim Palace in honor of the men of these regiments who were only just now returning home. It would be attended by a great number of distinguished people, possibly the biggest social event of the year, if not the decade. Famous men and women from other countries who happened to be in Britain or in Europe had also agreed to attend. She had an invitation herself and she invited me to accompany her. She then showed me the invitation, beautifully engraved and embossed, with two green dragons facing each other across a shield, topped by a lion standing on a red crown.

"Will you come?" she asked, her eyes both smiling and hopeful through the lenses.

"Will I come? Will I come! You bet I'll come! – and I'll get the best suit of evening clothes you ever saw!"

We spent the rest of that evening together in my rooms, drinking the champagne, slowly and appreciatively. It was, said the label, Vilmart 1902 which meant little to me or to my taste. We looked through my shelves of books and Madge was interested in the Stoddard lecture. I explained that a man I had met in London had recommended I should look out for more. She opened it, read, and nodded. I then read Whitman to her and she read some speeches from Shakespeare, including one or two of his sonnets.

"*No, Time, thou shalt not boast that I do change,*" she read, and I tried to lock the words into my brain.

"You are in love," she said suddenly.

"Yes."

"Will you tell me?"

So I told this fine woman friend, this Oxford blue-stocking, all about Daisy and our firm loyalty of love. I said nothing of the transformation of Jimmy Gatz but I did tell her that, of all the things that had ever happened to me, or that could ever be guessed to happen, this determined love was stronger than all other things combined or possible. I did not know then, of course, of the pain to come.

"Let me just say," she said, her face very close to mine, "that I wish you all the happiness in the world. You are a puzzle. A lovely, quiet and mysterious puzzle – but a puzzle all the same!"

We talked again of books and poetry.

"One of my favorites," she said, "one of the best of all time is Cervantes' *Don Quixote*. Do read it, Jay, re-read it, and read it again. Then start again from the beginning. It is a truth of men. They will read books, or newspapers, or comic books, or even see the silent movies, and then go forth to quarrel and to fight.

"There will be no more major wars now, of course, not now, impossible. But some man, some nation or people, a century from now, twenty-nineteen, will be the then Quixotic fight-finder, scouring the world for yet another war, another combat, other killings – with some wretched little Sancho trailing loyally behind.

"It is what they do, what they are. Cervantes' tale is a parable."

She went to the shelves and took down one or two of my American authors.

I might note here that I acquired a translation ("*by Charles Jarvis Esq.*") of the Cervantes novel some time later. I read much of it quickly but I drew very different conclusions from those of Madge. The knight, for me, was a man with a dream and a purpose. He would not be deterred. Judged by others he may have been in error. To himself he was true – to Dulcinea devoted and sworn.

It was around ten o'clock on that night with Madge, possibly later, that Cadman came into my rooms to check. He did this for the lights, the curtains, the bed and the chamber pot. When he saw Madge stretched out on my sofa with a book of Mark Twain, *Roughing It*, he stared without moving and said, bluntly and with his seldom used country accent:

"Woz she doin' 'ere?"

"She's my guest, Cadman."

He took up the near-attention stance again.

"Young ladies are not allowed to be in rooms, sir, after Hall. I shall have to inform the Dean. Goodnight to you."

Would I be sconced for this, I wondered.

As we rushed together, Madge and I, towards the porters' lodge to leave the college in haste we met Norrington in the Front Quad.

"Whither away so fast?" he said laughing. Elegant in a striking light suit with wide lapels, a smart shirt and tie, his hair neatly combed to a parting on the left of his head – smart for some fine social occasion – he said a courteous good evening to Madge.

"Trouble," I told him anxiously. "Madge overstayed her allowed time in college apparently. Cadman says he'll have to report me to the Dean."

Norrington smiled: "Oh, the rules, the rules! Never mind. It isn't a crime to have a young lady in your rooms – and certainly not when you've been serving in the military as you have, Gatters. If I recall correctly, the fine is half a crown, two shillings and sixpence, and that's the end of the matter, rest assured. Goodnight to you both."

He was right, thank goodness. I knocked on Mr. Higham's door the following morning after breakfast. He called me in, looked up for a moment, half smiled and shook his head.

"Sorry about that, Gatsby. Cadman was only doing his duty. Fine is either half a crown or five bob, I can't recall. The Bursar'll tell you. Shut the door, please."

I paid the fine at once and heard no more about this infringement of the college rules.

Before the Blenheim Ball, Cusworth and many others performed what was to be a spectacular jazz concert against the modeled spires of Oxford in the chapel quad. It lasted for eight hours, through a whole afternoon and evening, and nobody seemed to tire of either the playing or the listening. There was very little room to dance in the quad but several couples – and Madge pulled me to my feet – did their best to move to the music.

A small upright piano was brought in, with drums, saxophone, trumpet, trombone and clarinet. Others came with their own instruments to join in for a while. Some of the music was vibrantly infectious and I laughed at the response to the wild and raucous, ever growing louder *Alexander's Rag Time Band.* There was *The Memphis Blues* and *The Saint Louis Blues*, *Beale Street Blues* (again) and *Dark Town Strutters' Ball. After You've Gone* was followed by the wonderful and new *Clarinet Marmalade* and then the

Royal Garden Blues. These are just the pieces I remember or had time to note. There was so much more and, subtly because of the music and its origin, I was proud once again to be American that day and proud of the voice of a new renaissance.

It was clear that men and women had come here from places other than Trinity. The musicians I had seen, including Mr. Turnbull, were there from St John's College, and Cecil Parke had come over from Merton College with a young lady called Sin (short, I discovered, for Cynthia). Nurses from the infirmary must have been invited too because Mayra, ecstatic with the music, suddenly saw me with her massive smile and begged me to dance the *coladeira* with her. The music, she said, does not matter, "it is the steps that count!"

Madge applauded gently after my clumsy performance and Wilson-Hughes, drunk I guessed by this time (it was eight o'clock), cheered, stamped, and clapped loudly and sarcastically. I crossed the quad and put a hand on his shoulder.

"Thanks again, old sport," I told him. "You are a credit to your college and to your country."

His fists actually clenched as I stepped away, noting also as I turned back through the cluster of laughing people, all exhilarated by the jazz, that Johnny Cusworth was now dancing an improvised kind of Charleston with Mayra. As I passed closely by them I was further stunned to hear Johnny speaking to her in Portuguese.

The sky was dark by the time the party ended, hours later. I had spent the last period sitting alone with Madge. There were quiet benches in the garden and from time to time we left the hectic crowd and recovered a cooling breath on the lawns.

"You will leave soon," she said, "I can tell. I hope you'll remember me. I think you must be the first American boy I have ever known – though not the first boy I have fallen in love with."

I was about to speak.

"No!" she said. "I fall in love quite frequently, you see – with books, and songs, and music, and paintings... I'm a lucky girl, you know? At Christmas I met a woman called Sylvia Pankhurst. I was in London and she was setting up cost-price restaurants in the worst-off districts so that those who had no food or money could eat. I'm not like that, I'm afraid. I'm a scholarly blue-stocking and I intend to fight for women's rights here in Oxford, here with the university and, I hope, maybe teach other women everything I know.

"But the eagerness must be there, like Sylvia Pankhurst. We must, must, must, Jay Gatsby, do things with this century that cannot be unraveled or destroyed! I sense in you that singleness of mind, sweet man. That is why I fell in love with you. She is a lucky girl your Daisy. I was a Daisy once, you know," she added laughing.

The music ended at last. People sighed and breathed, mopped brows with linen handkerchiefs, dabbed cheeks with gentle powder, stretched collars with their fingers, stamped their feet for circulation, kissed and hugged, spoke in their high shrill Oxford tones, so many "darlings" now, shawls pulled across shoulders, drained glasses, coins given – crowns or sovereigns – to the scouts, the servants, who had come out to clear the mess. The piano was rolled away through the chapel arch. The instruments were wiped and placed with care into their cases.

Mayra was with other nurses (or so I guessed) standing in a cluster by the Hall doorway. Cusworth came up to me, as bright and cheery as ever, though hot and wet and pink.

"You know Mayra, old sport," he said, with a nod in her direction. "Some girl, eh! She kept calling you Jimmy for some reason – must have got mixed up. Some girl, eh?" he said again, and slapped me on the back. He was so warm, and open, and true, this man, as though I had been his friend or brother from infancy.

I walked with Madge to the Lodge and we said goodnight. She had made me promise to hire or to buy white tie and tails for the Blenheim Ball. I promised I would, the very best. There was a taxicab in Broad Street which she took to Somerville. I dreamed of Madge that night, in cool and silver-green just like a siren. But also with gown and mortar board, lecturing to a class on the subject of Kierkegaard and Abraham. The scholar mermaid.

Soon afterwards there was another short letter from Daisy. One sentence struck me in particular:

"So please do come soon, my dearest Jay. The world is so full, so crowded I fear to lose my balance."

I promised myself that after Blenheim I would see the President and the Dean to arrange my departure from Trinity.

The Blenheim Ball, though it was so much more than that, will live forever in my memory – but, more importantly, it created a lasting aspiration which I was resolved to achieve in equal measure as a token of my creative love for Daisy. This despite what was to occur soon after. I bought the white tie, tails, white and stiff cut-down waistcoat, the patent shoes, immaculate cuff buttons and black silk socks, all from a shop in Turl Street. Dressed before the mirror in my rooms I felt both fraud and heir.

Like every other American I have ever met or ever known I knew that we Americans are here to observe the world and then to act upon it. I may have arrived in Trinity College like a foreigner, a stranger, a visitor, or a messenger – even a prospective buyer perhaps. The final issue would not be whether I belonged to Trinity. The outcome would have to be whether Trinity, and all the splendid people I had known or met, could fold comfortably into this American's dream and take their place there.

The Blenheim occasion, when it happened, I would have dismissed a year earlier as some preposterous fantasy, as the wild-hope madness of a seething mind, a drugged hallucination, if I had not actually and physically been involved in it myself, eyes wide open, astonishment agape.

Madge had insisted that we should travel to Blenheim in a horse-drawn carriage.

"I can easily arrange it, don't worry. Johnny Cusworth is a cousin of mine and he's somehow connected to the Duke of Marlborough. There will be no problem about the coach."

It was another golden evening when I walked in tie and tails through the chapel arch of Trinity, along the side of the lawns and trees of the front quad, past the porters' lodge where the horse and carriage were waiting beyond.

The horse itself shone – it must surely have been washed and brushed to a gleaming white. The coachman was in dark green livery trimmed with gold and with a flat-topped hat rounded with red ribbon, gold front buckle, and a small feather. He wore white trousers and gleaming boots. The carriage was open and Madge was there waiting and smiling – and indescribably beautiful. Whatever colors were her own, whatever cut of dress or neck was hers, whatever jewels or ornaments, whatever gloves, whatever perfume, whatever lipstick, powder or eye shadow, whatever of these would most suit her and enhance her natural beauty were there – all brought together.

"You look gorgeous," she said to me as I climbed into the carriage.

We drove from Broad Street to St Giles then up and along the Woodstock road. The clopping of the white horse's hooves registered their rhythm in my head, making me foolishly and stupidly want to sing in tune. Madge held my hand as we travelled by small woods of dipping sunlight, trees overhung the roadway, birds perched on the branches and stared as we passed, one or two shouted down, on each side were open meadows, small cottages where sometimes leaning parents, at their doors with their children, pointed to us and waved and laughed and even called out *hooray*!

As we approached and entered Woodstock – a place I had visited more than once alone by bicycle – we pulled to the side and prepared to enter the gates of Blenheim Palace.

"It's the Duke of Marlborough, right?" I asked Madge.

"Right! There'll be others of course, I mean dozens! People with titles – and remember that, in a sense, this is all for you and for the soldiers. They'll be coming from all over – many from Oxfordshire, of course, but from London and everywhere in Britain, even from abroad, and from all sorts of different circles. So stand by, major!" She was full of brightness and mirth at the prospect.

"What do we do?"

"We stay patient. Most important. We line up to get out of the carriage. Then we walk into the Palace. Then we are presented to the Duke and the Duchess – she is

American by the way, and they got married in New York. I can tell you a bit more too, just: like you, he was in the army during the war, a Lieutenant Colonel, and he was at Trinity, but Cambridge."

"Isaac Newton?"

"Before his time."

It was as Madge had said: we waited for almost half an hour before arriving at the main entrance of the palace. Sitting in the open carriage I could only marvel at the extraordinary richness of the grounds, the lake, the gardens, the carefully planned distant vistas, and the overwhelming force and majesty of the palace itself.

As we stepped from the carriage, and as a young boy in uniform guided the horse away towards the stables, Madge said, "I also managed to get a confidential list of some of the guests. Once we're inside I'll try to let you know who's who." She winked.

We made a line along with at least eighty other new arrivals to be welcomed by the Duke and his lady. He was a gentleman of about fifty years of age, with tidy hair, left-side parted, and a small neat moustache. Rightly dressed, I thought as I drew closer, he would not be out of place with a saxophone in a Manhattan jazz club.

All the names were called in turn by a bold-voiced man in a white wig, silk embroidered costume, a lace at his neck and a strong staff in his hand. I was described as "Major Jay Gatsby of the First Division, American Expeditionary Forces!" Madge was announced as "The Honorable Margaret Curzon Wellesley!"

The Duke and Duchess shook our hands with sincere warmth, saying how welcome we were and that he, the Duke, must in particular thank all of us from America for our courage and our commitment. His wife, a lady in her forties, was extremely pretty. She said, in a beautiful and (for me) nostalgic accent: "It is a great pleasure to meet you, Major Gatsby. I hope that you and your lady will have a wonderful time here."

We had no sooner passed along the line of reception than the gentleman in the silks and wig banged his staff on the floor and proclaimed:

"Your grace, my lords, ladies and gentlemen, please welcome the men of the Queen's Own Oxfordshire Hussars and those of the Second Battalion of the Oxford and Buckinghamshire Light Infantry."

Two files of smartly uniformed men, most with ladies on their arms, walked into the Great Hall, the huge pillared and arched room where we now stood below the painted ceilings. They saluted as they passed the Duke and he raised an arm of greeting to each one.

As guests continued to arrive, Madge drew me away to an upholstered seat out of the general arena, to one side and quite concealed. She drew a rolled paper from her bag and whispered:

"See how many I recognize!"

I watched the guests walk from the presentation into the body of the Great Hall. Music, classical waltz, was already playing in another room and some of the guests passed immediately before us as they went towards the dance.

"That's Austen Chamberlain," Madge told me, "and I think that's Sir Arthur Henderson. There's Lord Birkenhead and just behind him is the painter John Singer Sargent. That's Mr. and Mrs. Cornfield who are something important here in Woodstock, and so is the young lady with them,

Diana Harcourt. I think she may be a suffragette but I'm not sure. I've certainly seen her picture in a newspaper.

"The man in the old-style breeches in Sir Maxim Denderfield from Witney and the woman just coming after him is the actress, Ellen Terry. I think that must be Mr. Arthur Balfour and his sister..."

It was. The same friendly host I had met in the box at *The Mikado*. He did not see us as they passed together towards the dance.

"Goodness," she exclaimed, "those two together! Look! Look! Mr. Bernard Shaw and Mr. Harley Granville Barker! I didn't think men like that would be guests for Blenheim Palace! And you see that young boy there? I saw him in *Charley's Aunt*, he is Master Noel Coward, a great child-actor, and I have a feeling he may be playing in pantomime somewhere. Pity he'll outgrow it all though. Oh and the woman there is from Somerville – she's determined that the college should become officially recognized, degrees and all. I think behind her that's the Master of Balliol and his wife. Yes, and there is the Warden of New College, and the Provost of Oriel – and it looks as if the Dean of Christ Church and the Rector of Lincoln have come together with their guests.

"That one is certainly Clara Butt, there in the blue dress with her husband, the baritone Mr. Kennerley Rumford – and, not surprising but it's good to see he is in better health, there's Sir Edward Elgar. Mr. Winston Churchill is just behind him with his wife, Clementine. She is American too by the way, Jay.

"That young man just over there is the painter Lucien Pissarro, son of Camille whom you may have heard of, and with him is another artist called Augustus John. They stick around in London together. Love the French impressionists, I think. Not sure though. There, of course, is the President of Magdalen.

"The two young men together with the orange badges are the Wilkin twins from Chipping Norton – they do great things with the young scouts. Oh, and that young lady trying to get through between them must be Miss Sybil Thorndike. Yes, it is! She's just pushed forward to Shaw and Granville Barker and they are hugging each other like birds of a feather. Shaw will probably write for her one day. Unlikely to be up to her standard though.

"Just look at that, Jay Gatsby!"

Something like thirty young ladies, identically dressed in the shimmery fringed dresses, cloche hats, long beads and high heels, were all approaching the Duke and Duchess together. Madge looked down her list of guests.

"Yes! There they are! It's all the girls from the cast of *Oh Joy!* at the Kingsway Theatre. I saw it, Jay, it's fun! Wodehouse and Kern and you cannot say better than that. Gosh! There they are! That's Mr. P.G. Wodehouse and Mr. Jerome Kern – and they've got Guy Bolton with them! Whatever next! And look! There's Hermione Gingold and, just in front of him, Ernest Rutherford who has just won the Nobel Prize for chemistry. Isn't this wonderful?"

She paused briefly for breath, eyes shining.

"I thought so," she went on, "there's your President, Trinity, I mean, Mr. Blakiston, and he's with..." she looked at the list.

"It's the Dean," I said, "Tommy Higham."

Again they walked by us without noticing.

The orchestral music was still playing in a nearby room, now Strauss, but further off, from the outside, we heard a jazz band strike up. We stayed for another quarter of an hour or so as Madge gave me more from the listed names of guests. At one point she thought she saw Charlie Chaplin – but it was a performer I did not know called Robey ("He'll be at the Royal Command for sure" Madge told me) and William Morris, whose poem I had noted at *The Thirteen Club*–but no! he was "not the same man" (Madge corrected). He was responsible for the Bull Nosed Morris automobiles which I had noticed weeks before.

"He's made four hundred this year so far. And growing. He's transforming Oxford and challenging Austin. He'll be very, very rich one day."

Would Gatsby make motors? I guessed not as the words she spoke caused me to consider the idea.

"Goodness me," she said under her breath, "I do believe that is Signor Antonio Scotti who used to be at the Royal Opera House in Covent Garden – and no! It can't be! Jay, look, Jay! Would you recognize Enrico Caruso if you saw him? It can't be!"

Many more arrived to form the line up to the Duke and Duchess and at last Madge grew tired of what she called her "little game".

For what followed we spent most of the hours outside the Palace itself, listening to the jazz in the gardens – again Madge sang, again I unsuccessfully tried the Charleston but I did reasonably well with a spiced up foxtrot (as she called it). It was a warm evening and all around the lawns and gardens were thousands of balloons with flamboyant decorations and, as it grew a little darker, some tasteful yet vividly explosive fireworks hit the sky above distant groves of lime trees and firs. There were more people in Blenheim than I could count: several hundred finally, and they mixed together amiably and informally – to my slightly prejudiced surprise about the English and their tiered society. Food of an unlimited variety and taste was spread out in all parts of the halls and rooms on long tables where people thronged together, and also across the lawns, in gardens and by the lakes: meats, fish, baked dishes, cold salads, cooked and fresh fruits, dishes made with eggs, shell fish in abundance, puddings, biscuits, cookies, jell-O with cream, jams and marmalades, and the mysterious puffy hillocks you find on all party plates which we bite in ignorance and swallow in hope.

There were at least one hundred young and not so young men and ladies in smart domestic uniforms serving the guests. Champagne poured freely and endlessly and people drank without inhibition. The soldiers in uniform were especially greeted with warmth. They danced with their ladies but the girls from the London musical were very popular. They danced with everyone.

Cusworth came to join us for a while, hand in hand with Mayra. Three of the chorus line girls were with them too and Johnny introduced them as Rita, Betty, and Eve.

"If you haven't danced the shimmy with one of these gals, you will not have lived, old sport."

I declined as courteously as I could, but later I did see Lord Birkenhead moving with a fair amount of grace in front of the energetic and laughing young Betty. P.G. Wodehouse, if I am correct the writer of the musical, danced with Rita, Eve, Clara Butt, and Sybil Thorndike.

We were asked at one point in the later evening, by men in uniform with loudspeakers, to return to the Great Hall "for a very special program", the hall having been transformed into a dazzling ballroom with a concert platform.

A complexity of lights, candles, flares and florescent drapes was everywhere. Hundreds now sat or stood together, cabinet ministers and chorus girls, scientists and nurses, the soldiers from the Oxford regiments, writers and poets, and though I cannot be sure of the names and the identities I seem to recall that it was Clara Butt who sang verses from *Land of Hope and Glory:*

> *Dear Land of Hope, thy hope is crowned,*
> *God make thee mightier yet!*
> *On Sov'reign brows, beloved, renowned,*
> *Once more thy crown is set.*
> *Thine equal laws, by Freedom gained,*
> *Have ruled thee well and long;*
> *By Freedom gained, by Truth maintained,*
> *Thine Empire shall be strong.*

After that, if Madge had been right about Enrico Caruso, then it was he who sang *La donna è mobile* followed by *Love or Fancy* together with Antonio Scotti ("from *Madame Butterfly*", Madge informed me.) There followed several orchestral pieces after which the Great Hall was given over to formal dances, and I watched as the elegance of England, and elsewhere, danced Viennese Waltzes, polkas, and some of the English and Scottish folk dances I had never known or heard of, one of them I think was called *The Dashing White Sergeant*. It was a relief that we soon got back to the jazz.

I tried to take such personal notes as I could, as so many of the people I met and spoke with were of lasting interest. I learned that the painter John Singer Sargent was at work on a family portrait for the Duke, but more arresting for me was what he told me of the journey he had made to work on his painting, *Gassed*.

"I had gone for that very purpose," he said, "to see and to understand. We had had tea and then went on to a place called Bac-du-Sud where there were dozens of gassed men – no, several hundred. I had been commissioned by the British Government. I thought they might reject the painting when I'd finished it. They have not, and it is to be there for a Hall of Remembrance."

Winston Churchill made a point of introducing himself, "to an American cousin." He was in the mid-forties, confident in that particular English way I saw in Cusworth and found so benevolent. He asked simply: "What do you do next, major?"

"Back home," I said. "Marriage – we've already waited too long. Then work. I shall need to make money."

That was, of course at the time, my total belief in what the future held.

"Politics? Our countries are going to need each other over the coming decades," Churchill said.

"I doubt if that is for me, sir," I replied. "I have very few objectives, but I mean to achieve them at any cost. Politics, I fear, is not among them."

"We need soldiers in government," he replied. "They know the world. Think about it, major. President Gatsby one day? Why not?"

He laughed as we parted but I sensed, yet again, that this forecast was not made altogether frivolously.

Introduced to Ernest Rutherford I begged him to explain the latest science he was working on and he said something like this: "I am bombarding nitrogen atoms with alpha rays to see a change in outgoing photons and if nitrogen converts to oxygen." I thanked him for the information and went in search of Madge who had excused herself to talk with P.G.

Wodehouse, now happily sipping champagne. Others I met I have not forgotten, though the details are less precise. I was with Madge or Cusworth for much of the time but also, walking, feeling, I absorbed for several hours this unprecedented vigor of life, this dazzle, performance, excitement and, above all, these people. At the end of the evening I was overwhelmed and overcharged with a new emotion of resolve.

The carriage was to wait for us down the drive towards Woodstock. Madge, I saw when she joined me to leave together, had refreshed her perfume and her make-up. The dark but country-scented journey back to Oxford was perfect as a fine seal for the night. We got out of the coach together outside Somerville – "I shall walk the rest," I said.

"Goodnight, Jay. Thank you for... for your friendship. Take care of the man you are – for my sake and for others. You are not just anything, you know." She kissed me lightly on the right cheek and disappeared into the college.

I walked along dark gas-lit St Giles, past *The Bird and Baby* and *The Randolph*, back along the Broad Street, and, as had been arranged, signaled my arrival to the night porter. The late hour was sanctioned as permissible by the nature of the event.

Some days later came the fatal letter from Daisy.

I did not know this until after a special memorial service that the President had arranged in the chapel. He was to read the full list of all the Trinitarians, one by one, who had been involved in the war, the Roll of Honor.

Much moved, I had also agreed, at his suggestion, to read some verses along with Dean Higham and my fellow undergraduate, Gerald Gent–verses from a poem written by Laurence Binyon in Cornwall in 1914 and published, I was told, in *The Times* newspaper.

The President began with a special address for the occasion and then read the names out, carefully, slowly, and with a deep respectful attention to each one, each individual. As I watched and listened I admired this man so much at this time – an unpretentious and withdrawn scholar, devoted to his college, to its people, and to all that these involved.

Everyone was silent and nobody moved. I had been asked to read first, as an American guest and friend-in-arms, and I stepped up to the lectern to the left of the chapel entrance. I read:

> "'They went with songs to the battle, they were young.
> 'Straight of limb, true of eye, steady and aglow.
> 'They were staunch to the end against odds uncounted,
> 'They fell with their faces to the foe.'"

I stepped down and Tommy Higham took my place. He read:

> "'They shall grow not old, as we that are left grow old:
> 'Age shall not weary them, nor the years condemn.
> 'At the going down of the sun and in the morning,
> 'We will remember them.'"

He in turn moved away and the undergraduate, Lieutenant-Colonel Gerald Gent, took his place. He too read:

> "'They mingle not with their laughing comrades again;
> 'They sit no more at familiar tables of home;
> 'They have no lot in our labour of the day-time;
> 'They sleep beyond England's foam.'"

There was silence. Prayers were said by the Chaplain. The President said he had one final announcement:

"We are seeking together the best and most lasting War Memorial for those we have just honored. Ideas will be circulated. It has been suggested that a Memorial Library should be built and I should mention the generosity of contribution which has already promised for this proposal. Much remains to be done."

The Chaplain gave a final blessing and we left the chapel without speaking a word to each other.

Daisy's letter was in my pigeon hole.

"Dear, dearest, darling Jay, how shall I tell you this?"

I shall never be able to express the feelings I endured as I read her words. The only far-fetched and inadequate way in which I can, even for myself, hold the impression of what happened to me is to imagine that I was to rise one morning early only to find that the sky was still dark, and then to wait hour after hour for signs of the sun, to wait on and on, and to find alarm, fear and disbelief that the sun would never rise again, that darkness was all, and forever.

That was something of how it was for me.

"The world is so full of noise," she wrote, "and people. I have loved you so much, Jay Gatsby, and thought of you so often. The world has been a swirl and a sweet fever for so long, you see. The need grew in me for strength and certainty. I must be honest and give you the truth.

"I have become engaged to be married, Jay. Please try to understand. I know you can. He is a strong and wholesome man who says he is devoted to me and will take all the care I can ever need with his power and his wealth. His name is Tom Buchanan and I know that I can trust him always, and that you, dearest Jay, will share the pleasure of my certainty.

"What we have had together will never be forgotten. Please think kindly of me, Jay. With affection, Daisy."

I walked alone for several days through the lanes of Oxfordshire, sleeping in the open, soaked by rain, hungry.

In our days of living some balm is usually apprehended in even the coldest night and the sun also rises. This was not so for me when I returned, finally and for the last time, to Trinity College.

I wrote a letter to Daisy. It said everything I felt for her, all that we could be together, all my pain and the darkness. It would take time to reach her, I knew, but I put it in the post.

Another disturbing message was waiting for me at the lodge: an official order from the American Military. Technically I was still under orders for several months. I should return to France, I was instructed, to take part in ceremonies in the territory which I had helped to liberate. Uniform and pay would be allocated and I was to take no resources of my own. The aim, I understood, was to reenact the final hours of the war and I was to be again as I had been then.

This had a terrible and painful appropriateness: a return to poverty and to the pre-Oxford Gatsby, a return to the battlefields and the slaughter, a return to the memory of Chuck Deacon and many others. This time, however, no light would lie ahead. The first time there had been the light of Daisy and the worth of living. Afterwards I would return to America as the poor soldier I had been. I would go to Louisville to retrace the fallen heart that was. And then?

"I have had bad news, I'm afraid." I said the same words to the Dean and to the President. They were both kind and warm, made no enquiries, shook my hand. I still had money from the scholarship and from the residue from Walter Chase. I would take little or nothing with me to France. I would be penniless again – until France and Louisville were behind me for a second time.

I packed my few belongings and arranged for the consignment of all my books to be delivered to the address in Whitehall Street, Manhattan, to await my collection sometime in the future. I took what remained of the money from under the carpet of my room, determined to spend it all within days to induce the temporary poverty I intended for France and Louisville. I said goodbye to Cadman and asked him not to come to my room in the morning, that I would prefer to wake myself and to leave quietly.

I said goodbye to many I had known in Trinity, to the helpful Norrington and to the heroic Gerald Gent. I also wished Wilson-Hughes the best for his future. He seemed to soften and shook my hand, twice, and with a fraternal pat on the back said, "all the best, whoever you are."

In his rooms Johnny Cusworth jumped from his chair with delight, grabbed my hand, and said that I must have seen *The Times* already that day. I told him that I had not and he waved a page in front of me. There I read that the Viscount John Mansfield Denham Rupert Cusworth, eldest son of His Grace the Earl of Doncaster, was engaged to be married to Miss Mayra Fonseca of Praia, Santiago, in the Cape Verde. He was engaged to marry Mayra! For a moment the joy of these two extraordinary friends together may have stopped my breath.

"That is wonderful, old sport," I said sincerely. "She will make a wonderful Countess."

"Quite right, old sport," he said with a slight frown. "And, sad so say, that could be at any time now."

He embraced me warmly like an Italian – or a Portuguese – and we promised somehow, someday to meet in Greenwich Village, he, myself and Mayra and "we'll show 'em the *coladeira*, what? I know just the place!"

I left my bed in the middle of that last Trinity night and went once more to the garden.

I felt that I had come a long way to these blue lawns from the ragged boy of North Dakota, the sailor with Cody, the scared lieutenant under German fire, the new and richer Gatsby, and the dream that had always been there before me. I stretched out on the grass once more and may have dozed for a moment. There was a moon that night and the light of stars. The days I had spent in solitude roaming the Oxfordshire lanes had persuaded me that after all my quest was by no means over. Daisy had been caught up in a young girl's need for safety and for wealth and for the social things she loved and needed. Yet she loved me still and most of all, of that I was certain.

I resolved once more to go to France, return to the old poverty for the time being, see Louisville once more as a penniless youngster, but then to begin the massive work which, thanks to Meyer Wolfshiem, I would undertake for many months to come. I would amass a fortune, the most enormous fortune I could imagine and which, I knew, would win Daisy back to me from whoever Tom Buchanan was or whatever he could give her. It did not matter how I would do this.

Then, rich, if required, I would build a Blenheim Palace just for her. It would be a place of astounding light and sound, ever open, ever splendid. I would be the greatest host that America had ever known. I would lay all this at her feet and make her see that love we had and have, was, and is, and will remain stronger and more forceful than anything which could oppose it, anything she could ever find elsewhere. I would do all this and I would never fail.

As I lay there in that Oxford night, on the lawns of Trinity, clouds sliding one by one across the path of the moon, I distinctly heard and saw once more, though for the last time, the shimmering siren at the depth of the garden, silver and green, and I heard the high song once again. This time I believed I could understand the meaning of the words: that I should love and have no doubts, that I should do all that I must and like the Dutch sailors on the coasts of their new world, I should allow my wonder of expectation to drive my courage and my trust to uncompromising conquest. You will be rich, I thought she sang, the mermaid, vanishing.

I left my room next morning and saw no-one as I walked towards the Lodge with my luggage. The porter may have waved, I cannot be sure. I crossed the Broad Street and walked down what Oxford people called the Turl towards the High Street.

Half way along the Turl, at the corner of Brasenose Lane and Lincoln College, I stopped and turned. This was to be my last sight of Trinity College. Foolish perhaps, but I put down my bag, stood to attention and saluted. There was the front quad, the chapel tower, and the gates which I would see no more.

It was the final closing of my Trinity story. I would tell it to nobody but keep such memories of the events and people I had known locked and excluded in my own archival mind. From now on I was to be Gatsby, the all-American hunter. Once I was back from the relived poverty of France and Louisville, a vast fortune, my own Blenheim Palace, and the rescue of Daisy were to be my total definition, all that would be known of me.

I supposed that if anyone, later, were to tell my story it

would be the tale of a mysterious and determined Gatsby and his solo mission for Daisy Fay. Oxford, unfairly perhaps to those I knew, would scarcely be heard of again. Even then only with doubt and disbelief.

On the High Street I crossed and looked into the window of *Hall Brothers* but what I sought was no longer there. I pushed the door and entered. The same short man with pince-nez approached me, a tape measure still around his neck but now broadly smiling.

"I was so sure that you would be back, sir," he said. "I thought it would be such a shame if you missed it. It is so right for you, sir, so absolutely right! It suits you perfectly."

He pulled a box from under the counter, smiling more broadly than ever.

"Here we are, sir," he said. "I saved it for you."

An echo, as from the future, a triple incentive, spoke to me: Daisy! Daisy! Daisy!

I bought the gold hat.